TRIMA   D
OTHE

To find out more about the Roman Mysteries, visit
www.romanmysteries.com

THE ROMAN MYSTERIES
by Caroline Lawrence

Also available

The Code of Romulus

The First Roman Mysteries Quiz Book

The Second Roman Mysteries Quiz Book

— A Roman Mystery —

TRIMALCHIO'S FEAST AND OTHER MINI-MYSTERIES

Caroline Lawrence

Orion
Children's Books

First published in Great Britain in 2007
by Orion Children's Books
a division of the Orion Publishing Group Ltd
Orion House
5 Upper St Martin's Lane
London WC2H 9EA

An Hachette Livre UK Company

3 5 7 9 10 8 6 4 2

A catalogue record for this book is
available from the British Library

ISBN 978 1 84255 593 4

Printed in Great Britain by Clays Ltd, St Ives plc

www.orionbooks.co.uk

To Steven Saylor, whose wonderful short stories inspired me to try some of my own

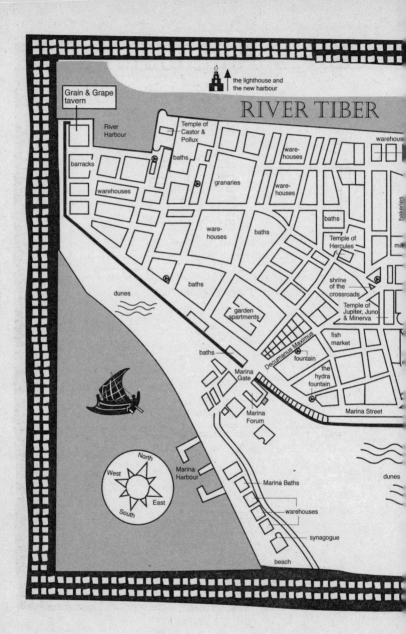

the lighthouse and
the new harbour

RIVER TIBER

Grain & Grape
tavern

River
Harbour

Temple of
Castor &
Pollux

barracks

baths

warehouses

warehouses

warehouses

granaries

ware-
houses

baths

warehouses

Temple of
Hercules

dunes

ware-
houses

baths

shrine
of the
crossroads

baths

Temple of
Jupiter, Juno
& Minerva

garden
apartments

fish
market

Decumanus Maximus

baths

fountain

Marina
Gate

the
hydra
fountain

Marina
Forum

Marina Street

North

West

Marina
Harbour

Marina Baths

dunes

East

South

warehouses

synagogue

beach

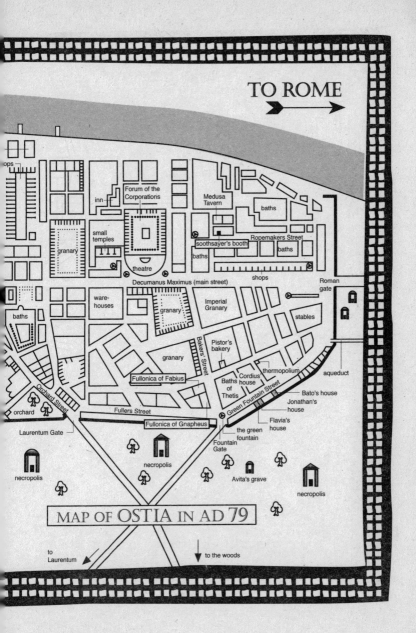

TO ROME

shops

inn

Forum of the
Corporations

Medusa
Tavern

baths

small
temples

granary

soothsayer's booth

Ropemakers Street

theatre

baths

baths

shops

Decumanus Maximus (main street)

Roman
gate

ware-
houses

granary

Imperial
Granary

stables

baths

granary

Pistor's
bakery

aqueduct

Bakers' Street

Fullonica of Fabius

thermopolium

Cordius
house

Baths
of
Thetis

Orchard Street

orchard

Fullers Street

Green Fountain Street

Bato's house

Jonathan's
house

Fullonica of Gnapheus

Flavia's
house

Laurentum Gate

necropolis

Fountain
Gate

the green
fountain

necropolis

Avita's grave

necropolis

MAP OF OSTIA IN AD 79

to
Laurentum

to the woods

CONTENTS

INTRODUCTION

by Caroline Lawrence

The incidents in the Roman Mysteries series take place during the two-and-a-half-year reign of the emperor Titus. He becomes emperor in the first book, *The Thieves of Ostia*. His mysterious death in AD 81 will be the subject of the final mystery, *The Man from Pomegranate Street*. Each of the books in between occurs at a specific point in the timeline of Titus's short reign. For example, *The Secrets of Vesuvius* takes place in July and August of AD 79, in the weeks leading up to the eruption of Vesuvius. *The Enemies of Jupiter* takes place in February of AD 80, when we know there was a terrible plague and fire in Rome. The Flavian amphitheatre (or 'Colosseum' as it is known today) was officially opened in the spring of AD 80, shortly after the plague and fire, so *The Gladiators from Capua* is set in March.

Some of the books in my series follow hard on each other. *The Pirates of Pompeii* takes place immediately after *The Secrets of Vesuvius*. *The Gladiators from Capua* resolves the cliff-hanger ending of *The Enemies of Jupiter*. But some books take place a few months apart. I am sometimes asked what Flavia and her friends were doing during the summer months between the events of *The Charioteer of Delphi* (September AD 80) and *The Slave-girl from Jerusalem* (December AD 80).

Some careful readers of the Roman Mysteries ask me questions like 'Who is Porcius?' or 'What happened with the monkey at Lupus's ninth birthday?' or 'Will we ever find out what happened to Silvanus from *The Colossus of Rhodes*?'

I even plant clues in the books which I can flesh out in future stories. At the beginning of *The Enemies of Jupiter*, Jonathan makes a reference to the disaster that was Lupus's birthday party. I purposely put that in before I wrote *Trimalchio's Feast* knowing that one day I would have the pleasure of writing about Lupus's ninth birthday.

This collection of short stories – or mini-mysteries – will help fill some of the gaps in the books and answer some of your questions.

Caroline Lawrence

These mini-mysteries take place in Ancient Roman times, so a few of the words may look strange.

If you don't know them, 'Aristo's Scroll' on pages 115-122 will tell you what they mean and how to pronounce them.

THE CASE OF THE
MISSING COIN

**This short story takes place in July AD 79,
between book I, *The Thieves of Ostia*, and book II,
The Secrets of Vesuvius.**

'Flavia!' called Alma. 'There's someone here to see you!'

Flavia Gemina had just settled herself on a branch of the fig tree in her inner garden. 'Who is it, Alma?' she called, without looking up from her scroll.

Alma – a cheerful, well-padded house-slave – must have gone back into the kitchen because her reply was indistinct.

Flavia scowled, rolled up the papyrus scroll and carefully balanced it on a smaller branch.

'*Who's* here to see me?' she yelled from the green depths of the tree.

Alma's reply sounded like: 'Pandora.'

That couldn't be right.

Flavia carefully stood up on the smooth branch and pushed aside the big heavy leaves. On hot summer days like this, the fig tree was her favourite place. Fig trees gave the deepest, coolest shade and this one had the added benefit of a splashing fountain just beneath it. Hers was one of the wealthier houses in the Roman port of Ostia; most people lived in apartment blocks or in rooms above shops.

'*Who*?' she directed her voice towards the kitchen.

'Flavia!' It was her father's voice, coming from behind her. Flavia turned and leaned forward and parted the leaves on the other side of the tree.

Her father stood in the doorway of the tablinum, looking up at her with his hands on his hips.

'Flavia Gemina,' he said. 'How many times have I asked you not to bellow? I'm raising you to be a proper Roman lady, not a fishwife! And please come down out of that tree. You're not a child any more. You are ten years old. In two years you'll be of a marriageable age.'

'Sorry, Pater,' said Flavia. 'I didn't know you were home.'

'That's obvious,' her father muttered, and disappeared back into the tablinum.

Flavia sighed and scrambled down from the tree. It was a blistering hot July afternoon. Outside, in the graveyard, the cicadas creaked slowly. Caudex the door-slave had gone to the ice-merchant, her tutor Aristo was at the baths and her personal slave-girl Nubia was walking the dogs outside the city walls. Flavia had been looking forward to a peaceful hour of reading her favourite Greek myths. She sighed again.

But when she saw the girl standing in the atrium by the rainwater pool, her irritation was replaced by curiosity.

Flavia guessed the stranger was the same age as she was. The girl wore a faded tunic of unbleached wool and leather sandals, one of which had been repaired with twine. Despite her poor clothes, it was obvious that the girl was not a slave: her dark hair was pinned up neatly and her posture was erect. The leather bulla around her neck was cheap, but it marked her out as freeborn.

'You must be Flavia Gemina,' said the girl politely. 'I'm Pandora.'

'Pandora, like in the Greek myth?' asked Flavia. 'That's a strange name.'

The girl nodded. 'It's my nickname.'

'It's not a very nice nickname,' said Flavia. 'Pandora opened a box that released sickness and death into the world.'

'I know,' said the girl. 'My real name is Didia Helpidis but my father calls me Pandora because my mother died giving birth to me. He says I caused all the evils in his life.'

Flavia gasped. 'What a terrible thing to say!'

'I hear you solve mysteries,' said Pandora quietly. 'I can't pay you. But I'm very good at mending. If you have—'

'No,' said Flavia. 'Don't worry about that. Why don't you tell me . . . Look, come up to my room. It's more private there. We can talk.'

Pandora nodded solemnly and Flavia led the way out of the atrium, through the inner garden and up the polished wooden stairs to the rooms on the upper floor.

Flavia sat cross-legged on her bed and gestured for Pandora to sit on the other bed.

Pandora looked down at her dusty toes in the open

5

sandals. 'I'll stand, if you don't mind,' she said, and added. 'I can't stay long.'

'Then let's not waste any time,' said Flavia. 'Tell me your mystery.'

'It's Briseis,' said Pandora.

'Briseis?' Flavia frowned. 'Isn't that the name of Achilles' girlfriend from *The Iliad*? I was just reading that.'

'Briseis is my father's slave-girl,' said Pandora. 'She hates me and she's always trying to get me in trouble. I think she hopes Pater will send me away, or even sell me to a slave-dealer. She wants him all to herself.'

Flavia realised her mouth was hanging open. She shut it and tried to compose her face into an expression of calm sympathy.

Pandora continued: 'This morning pater gave me a gold coin to take to the banker's stall in the forum. Briseis hates that he trusts me to run errands.'

'Your father lets you run errands in Ostia all alone? With no bodyguard?'

Pandora nodded. 'I like running errands. If I had to stay in and weave all day, I'd go mad with boredom.' Pandora sighed. 'Anyway, I left the coin on my bedside table and went to the latrine.

'When I came back, Briseis was standing right in the middle of my bedroom, as if she'd heard me coming. The first thing I thought was: she's stolen the coin. And when I looked at the table, I was right. The coin had gone.'

'Oh!'

Pandora looked at Flavia. 'I told Briseis to put the coin back. But she pretended not to know anything about it. She said "Coin? What coin? Oh dear, you haven't lost your father's gold coin have you? He'll be very angry and beat you, I suppose." But I could tell from her face she stole it. She only smiles like that when she's doing something mean to me.'

'Go on,' said Flavia.

'I said *she* must have taken the coin. But she opened her hands and there was nothing in them. She was wearing an unbelted tunic with no coin purse so she couldn't have hidden it on her person.'

'Does she have one of those complicated hairdos that all the fashionable women are wearing these days? You know, lots of curls piled high on the head?'

Pandora shook her head. 'No. Just thin straight hair. And when she's at home she doesn't even tie it back.' For the first time the girl's posture sagged. 'I know she's hidden the coin somewhere in my room, but I've looked everywhere and I can't find it.'

'Could she have swallowed it?' asked Flavia. 'I read that Cleopatra once pretended to drink a priceless pearl dissolved in vinegar but really she swallowed it whole and then retrieved it from the latrine bucket the next day.'

'Oh,' said Pandora. 'I didn't think of that. Maybe she did swallow it.' The girl covered her face with her hands.

'But I imagine an aureus would be much harder to swallow than a smooth round pearl,' said Flavia quickly. 'So let's assume she didn't swallow it. Shall we go back to your house and search your room? I'm very good at finding things . . . '

Pandora lifted her head and looked at Flavia. Her eyes were dry but red-rimmed. 'Pater doesn't let me have visitors. I waited until Briseis went out shopping before I came here. I was afraid she might take the coin from wherever she hid it in my bedroom. Then I'd never find it. Flavia, you must help me. If I don't give that coin to the bankers, Pater will find out and he'll beat me. And Briseis will gloat like she always does.'

'Don't worry, Pandora,' said Flavia, 'we'll just have to find the coin without going to your house. And I think I know how!'

'How can you find the missing coin if you aren't in the room?' asked Pandora, her dark eyes wide.

'Come and sit here,' said Flavia firmly, patting her bed.

Pandora sat on the bed but kept her dusty feet carefully on the floor.

Flavia handed Pandora a wax tablet and stylus. 'Make a list of every object in your room. Then we'll figure out where that nasty slave-girl might have hidden your father's gold coin.'

Pandora hung her head and murmured something.

'What?' said Flavia gently.

'I can't read or write,' said Pandora. 'Pater says girls don't need to be educated. He says women only need to know how to weave and be charming and keep their mouths closed.'

Flavia swallowed an angry remark and forced herself to speak calmly. 'Then *tell* me. Describe every object in your room. First of all, could Briseis have hidden the coin under a floorboard or in a crack in the plaster of the walls?'

'There's only one loose floorboard,' said Pandora, lowering her voice to a whisper: 'Under my bed. That's where I keep my treasures: a silver hairpin that used to belong to my mother, a little clay model of a horse and some pretty glass beads. That was the first place I looked after Briseis left the room. Thank Juno she doesn't know about it. The coin wasn't there.'

'Cracks in the plaster wall?' prompted Flavia.

'There are a few,' Pandora said. 'But they're too high to reach and they're very fine.'

'Any nooks or crannies?'

Pandora shook her head.

Suddenly the room grew dimmer as Alma appeared in the doorway. 'Brought you girls some barley water,' she said. 'Nice and cold. Caudex just got back from the ice-merchant.'

'Thank you, Alma,' said Flavia. She took the beakers and handed one to Pandora, who stared at it.

'It's delicious,' said Flavia. 'Try some.'

Pandora took a sip. 'Oh!' she cried. 'It's cold!'

'Go on,' urged Flavia. 'You were describing your bedroom.'

Pandora looked around. 'My room is small like yours,' she said. 'But not as nice. Mine has blank walls with no shelves. I have a chest like you but no dressing table or stool. And only one bed, with a little table beside it.'

'The window!' cried Flavia, pointing up at a small window with a latticework screen. 'Could she have tossed the coin out the window?'

'No,' said Pandora. 'I don't have a window. The only light comes through the doorway.'

'It must be quite dark,' said Flavia. 'And stuffy.'

'Yes,' said Pandora.

'You checked the mattress and shook out your blanket?'

'Yes. And I looked under the bed and through all the tunics and cloaks in my chest. Nothing there.' Pandora bit her lip.

'What's on your bedside table?' asked Flavia.

'A clay oil-lamp just like yours. A wooden comb,

some wooden hairpins. My beauty set. And a beaker for water. It's only copper, not glass,' she added.

'Do you have a chamber pot under the bed?' asked Flavia.

Pandora nodded. 'Yes, but I don't use it very much. It makes the room smell. I prefer to go down to the latrine. It's by the hearth in the kitchen.'

'So the pot was empty this morning?'

'Yes,' said Pandora.

'OK,' said Flavia. 'I'm going to search your room in my imagination.' She closed her eyes. 'I'm walking in. It's quite dim. I can see a bed there in the corner against the walls, a chest at the other end of it, a bedside table next to it, an empty chamber pot under it.' She opened her eyes for a moment. 'Nothing else in the room?'

'No,' said Pandora.

Flavia closed her eyes again.

'On your bedside table I see an oil-lamp, a comb and three hairpins—'

'Four.'

'Four hairpins, and a cup. Mirror?' Flavia opened her eyes. 'Do you have a mirror?'

Pandora shook her head.

'But how do you see yourself?'

'I don't.'

'You said you had a beauty set. Like this one?' Flavia reached over to her own bedside table, then held out a collection of bronze objects on a leather thong: an ear-scoop, a nail file, a tiny bottle of scented oil, and a pair of tweezers.

'Mine isn't as nice as yours. And it doesn't have the little bottle.' Pandora pulled out the tiny cork and sniffed. 'Mmm,' she said. 'It smells wonderful.'

'It's rose and myrtle oil.' Flavia closed her eyes again. 'Beauty set . . . No, couldn't hide a ring there. I see the copper beaker . . . was there water in it?'

'Yes, a little. But there was no coin at the bottom.'

Flavia kept her eyes shut and murmured to herself as she pretended to comb her hair, sip an imaginary drink, pick up the invisible oil-lamp. Suddenly her eyes opened wide.

'Pandora!'

'Yes?'

'Is your oil-lamp like this one?'

Pandora took the clay oil-lamp from Flavia. It was made of fired clay and had two holes: one at the end – for the wick, and one on top – to pour in the olive oil.

'Yes,' said Pandora. 'Mine is like yours.'

'Does your lamp have the four rabbits running round the hole for olive oil? Like this one?'

'Yes. We get our oil-lamps from Serapiodorus near the fish-market.'

'So the hole on top of your oil-lamp is the same

size as this one?' said Flavia. 'About the same size as a gold coin?'

Pandora looked down at the oil-lamp, then slowly up at Flavia. And for the very first time that day she smiled.

'Flavia!' called Alma. 'There's somebody here to see you!'

Flavia Gemina was sitting at the dressing table in her bedroom. She stopped combing her hair and opened her mouth. Then she remembered herself.

Letting her light brown hair fall loose around her shoulders, Flavia hurried downstairs to the atrium.

'Pandora!' she cried. 'I thought it might be you.'

The girl's eyes were shining.

'Flavia,' she said. 'The most wonderful thing.'

'What? Tell me!'

'When I got home yesterday Pater was furious with me. Briseis had just come in. She said she had seen me in the market, spending his gold coin on pastries, and she accused me of stealing things from her, too. I said, "No! Briseis is a liar! She hid the coin in my room this morning, and I can prove it." So I went upstairs and they followed me up and I went to the oil-lamp—'

'Pandora!' cried Flavia in horror, 'that was only a theory!'

'But Flavia!' said Pandora, and tears welled up in

her eyes, 'you were right! The coin was there! Inside the oil-lamp! It proved that Briseis was lying!'

Pandora gripped Flavia's hand and gazed into her face. 'Pater turned on Briseis and said he had suspected all along that she was untrustworthy and that was why he always asked me to go to the bankers. And she just stood there like a fish opening and closing her mouth. And he was so angry that yesterday afternoon he sold her at the slave-market and bought a new house-slave. One like yours.' Now Pandora was crying and laughing at the same time. 'And Flavia, she's *nice* to me!'

— AUTHOR'S NOTE —

Sometimes, when I do school visits, I bring in ancient and replica Roman artefacts to show the pupils. My most precious artefact is a real 2000-year-old clay oil-lamp from Roman Egypt. One day I was at a school and I held it up. Instead of telling the children what it was, I asked them to guess. Some of their guesses were silly: 'Please, Miss, is it a keyhole?'; 'Please, Miss, is it a shoe for a dwarf?' Others were sensible: 'Please, Miss, is it an inkwell?' 'Please, Miss, is it a musical instrument, like an ocarina?' Then one boy raised his hand. 'Please, Miss, is it for hiding things in?' I started to laugh and then stopped. The bigger hole is about the same size as an aureus, a gold coin of the first century AD. I know this because I have a set of replica Roman coins from the British Museum. One of them is an aureus of Domitian. I took this replica coin and held it over the bigger hole on the oil-lamp and let go. It dropped in. 'Brilliant suggestion!' I said to the boy. 'In fact, you've just given me a good idea.'

As soon as I got home, I sat down and wrote this short story.

TRIMALCHIO'S FEAST

This short story takes place in February AD 80,
between book VI, *The Twelve Tasks of Flavia
Gemina*, and book VII, *The Enemies of Jupiter.*

'Lupus! Stop that!' cried Flavia Gemina. 'You've been flicking balls of wax at us all morning and it's very annoying!'

Eight-year-old Lupus glared up at her from his writing tablet. He had no tongue so he could not speak.

'It's *extremely* annoying,' said Flavia's next-door-neighbour Jonathan without looking up from his own work.

'It vexes us,' agreed Flavia's ex-slave-girl Nubia, whose Latin was not quite fluent.

The four friends were having lessons as usual in the atrium of Flavia's house in the Roman port of Ostia.

'Lupus,' sighed their tutor, Aristo 'I must agree. Your behaviour this morning is very immature.' Aristo was a handsome young Greek with curly hair and long-lashed brown eyes.

'Yes.' Flavia waited until Aristo looked down at his scroll before picking some wax off the tip of her stylus, rolling it into a ball and flicking it at Lupus. 'Stop being so immature.'

Lupus's green eyes blazed with fury and the iron legs of his chair scraped against the black and white mosaic floor as he pushed away from the table. A few paces took him to the front door of the house. Two dogs emerged from beneath the table and wagged their tails hopefully as he lifted the heavy oak bar and opened the door.

'Lupus!' cried Aristo. 'Don't you dare walk out in the middle of lessons!'

Lupus's reply was to slam the front door behind him.

The two dogs padded back to the table with resigned looks on their faces.

'I wonder what's wrong with Lupus?' said Flavia, giving Scuto an absent-minded pat on the head.

'He's been in a bad mood for over a week,' Jonathan agreed.

'Maybe he is unwell.' Nubia scratched her dog Nipur behind the ear. 'Perhaps with fever.'

'But he's already had the fever,' said Flavia. 'We all have. Well, all except for you, Nubia.'

'Then maybe he is not liking this cold weather,' said Nubia, pulling her lionskin cloak round her shoulders. 'With the frost every morning and ice-skin on impluvium.'

'I don't think the cold bothers him,' said Jonathan. 'He goes out all the time without his cloak. Did I tell you he ran off two days ago, on the morning of the Sabbath? He didn't come back until after dark. Father was very worried.'

'What did you say to make him run off?'

'I'm not sure. I can't remember what we were talking about.'

'Maybe it is his tongue,' said Nubia. 'It must be most terrible not to have a tongue.'

'But his tongue was cut out over two years ago,' said Jonathan. 'He's probably used to it by now.'

'I don't think you'd ever get used to that,' said Aristo, and they were all silent for a few moments.

'Maybe he is missing his family,' said Nubia, who had seen her own family killed by slave-traders the previous year.

'Maybe,' said Flavia. 'It's definitely a mystery. And one I think we should solve.'

'I suggest you solve it after lessons are finished.' Aristo glanced up at the compluvium, the rectangular skylight in the ceiling. 'We still have a good two hours before noon and you haven't finished translating this passage from Latin into Greek.'

'Will you help us, Aristo?' asked Nubia. 'Will you help us solve the mystery of why Lupus is sad?'

'Not today. I'm going hunting this afternoon. It's Leander's birthday tomorrow and I wanted to give him a hoop of fig-peckers or a nice brace of hare. Maybe the day after tomorrow—'

'Birthday!' cried Jonathan. 'We were discussing Father's birthday next month. That's when Lupus ran off.'

Flavia frowned. 'I don't understand. Why should that upset Lupus?'

'Do you remember the day we found Lupus? After he fell out of the tree and we took him to my house?'

'Of course,' said Flavia. 'That was when we first discovered why he couldn't speak.'

'And remember when we asked him how old he was?'

Flavia nodded. 'He held up eight fingers and then waggled his hands—'

'—as if to say, "about eight years old".'

Flavia gasped. 'We've never asked him when his birthday is!'

Jonathan nodded. 'I'm sure that's it! That's why he's upset. We keep talking about other people's birthdays, but never about his.'

There was a pause and then Nubia said quietly, 'You are never asking when my birthday is also.'

'But . . . we . . . I never . . .' Words failed Flavia.

Aristo smiled and leaned forward. 'Nubia,' he said gently. 'When is your birthday?'

Nubia lifted her chin a fraction and said, 'I am born eleven and a half years ago in the centre of the month you call August.'

'Wait!' said Jonathan. 'If you'll be twelve next August . . . that means you're a month older than I am!'

'Nubia!' breathed Flavia. 'You'll be old enough to get married!'

Nubia glanced at Aristo and covered her hot face with her hands.

'So we think the reason Lupus is so upset,' said

Flavia quickly, 'is that we've never asked about his birthday.'

Jonathan shrugged. 'That's my theory.'

'Well then,' said Aristo. 'You'd better find out when he was born.' He smiled and tapped the papyrus scroll with his stylus. 'After lessons have finished.'

'I wonder,' said Flavia a few hours later, 'if Lupus even knows the date of his birthday.' It was drizzling lightly and the three friends stood beneath the shelter of a tall umbrella pine watching their three dogs romp in the dripping grove outside Ostia's town walls.

Jonathan nodded. 'And when people don't know the exact date of their birthday they usually celebrate it on the Kalends.'

'Kalends are the first day of month,' said Nubia. 'I know this.'

'That's right,' said Flavia. 'And tomorrow it will be the Kalends of February. I say we organize a birthday dinner party for Lupus, for tomorrow afternoon!'

'Good idea,' said Jonathan. 'Shall we have it at our house or yours?'

'Ours. We can make a big feast with all his favourite foods—'

'And music' said Nubia.

'Yes, and we can recline and wear birthday garlands—'

23

'And we can purchase for Lupus many fine gifts,' said Nubia.

'Yes,' said Jonathan. 'But what should we get him?'

'Eureka!' cried Flavia as Nipur ran up with a stick. 'I've got it! We'll get him a dog! I've often thought it a shame that we all have dogs but Lupus doesn't.'

'I'm not sure if Father would approve of another dog in the house,' said Jonathan. 'Last week Tigris chewed one of Father's favourite boots. Didn't you? You bad dog,' he ruffled the fur on Tigris's head affectionately.

'I am thinking another dog might cause big chaos,' said Nubia, tossing the stick back towards the town wall. The dogs raced after it.

Flavia sighed. 'You're right, of course. It's a bad idea.' She pulled her blue palla up to cover her head as they left the shelter of the trees.

'No,' said Nubia. 'It was not bad idea. Just dog part. But we could seek another pet for Lupus.'

'Yes!' cried Flavia. 'If he had his own pet he wouldn't feel left out.'

'There are some animal stalls at the market in the Marina Forum,' said Jonathan, pausing by his back door. His house, like Flavia's, was built into the town wall. 'Let's meet at the Marina Gate at the eighth hour, after we've been to the baths.'

'Good idea!' said Flavia. 'See you then!'

'Behold!' cried Nubia, clapping her hands. 'A scarab beetle!'

'A what?' said Flavia, moving closer to the stall.

The rain had stopped and the afternoon sun shone through a thin glaze of clouds, casting a pearly light over the Marina Forum. It was two hours after noon and they had all been to the baths.

'Scarab beetle.' Nubia pointed to a tiny ivory cage with an iridescent green beetle inside.

'These are special,' said the stallholder, a short olive-skinned man with an oiled beard. 'They will bring luck to your house.'

'It is like walking jewel,' breathed Nubia. 'Like emerald.'

'Ugh!' said Flavia. 'It's got all those little bug legs. And what does it need those pincers for anyway?'

'To roll balls of dung,' said Nubia.

'Balls of dung?' Jonathan raised an eyebrow.

Nubia nodded happily. 'Is he not beautiful? And behold the tiny cage is finely wrought. How much is he?'

'One hundred sesterces,' said the stallholder, and chuckled at their horrified faces. 'That's because the cage is made of ivory. Buy one with a wooden cage and they only cost three sesterces.'

'Oh, Flavia! I think Lupus would like this lucky jewel beetle.'

'I think so, too!' said Flavia, and to the stall keeper:

25

'We'll take one in a wooden cage!'

'Long live Caesar! Long live Caesar!' squawked a voice in the bird-market.

'Hark!' said Nubia. 'A bird is talking.'

Jonathan snorted. 'Birds don't talk.'

'Yes, they do!' said Flavia. 'It says so in Pliny's *Natural History*. There's a certain type of magpie that will talk if you feed it acorns. And Nero had a nightingale that could sing in Greek. Come on.' She led them through a forest of reed cages and twittering birdsong.

'Long live Caesar!' The croaking voice came from above them.

'Behold!' said Nubia. 'There is the bird who talks.' She pointed up at a small green and red bird in a wicker cage.

'Long live Caesar!'

'That bird isn't really speaking,' said Jonathan, tipping his head back. 'It must be some sort of trick.'

'No, it's really speaking, Jonathan.'

'Speaking Jonathan,' said the bird and Jonathan's jaw dropped.

'Siptax is a mimic,' said a dusky-skinned woman in clothing as colourful as the plumage of the birds around her. She had a long pole and used this to unhook the bird-cage and bring it down to their level. Jonathan took the cage and peered at the bird.

'He's from India,' continued the woman. 'His name is Siptax. He repeats whatever you say.'

Flavia looked at the price tag. 'We still have enough to buy him,' she whispered. 'Shall we?'

'We already have beetle,' said Nubia.

'But Lupus might be offended if all we get him is a bug. Even a pretty one,' she added hastily at the look on Nubia's face.

'I think Lupus would like this bird,' said Jonathan to the girls. 'Especially if we could train him to say "Happy Birthday, Lupus."' Jonathan turned back to the bird. 'Lupus,' he said, slowly and clearly. 'Lupus.'

The bird fluttered to a higher bar and then back down again.

'Lupus,' said Jonathan one more time. 'Say Lupus, you silly bird.'

'Silly bird!' squawked Siptax.

They all laughed and Jonathan nodded at the woman. 'We'll take him!'

'We still have a little money left over,' said Flavia as they passed through the Marina Gate back into Ostia. 'Let's go via the fish market and get Lupus some oysters. They're his favourite food.'

'I shall compose a special song for Lupus on my flute,' said Nubia.

'What a good idea! I'll write an "Ode to Lupus" to

go with your tune. Then we can perform it for him at the party.'

'Ah, the fish-market.' Jonathan inhaled deeply. 'You can always smell it before you see it.'

He led the way through an arch on the right, flanked by tall pink marble columns. The three friends emerged into a big bright courtyard, open to the overcast sky.

'Oh,' said Flavia, looking around. 'All the stalls have closed. We should have come this morning.'

'There is one shop still open,' said Nubia, pointing to a shop with the wooden shutters only half rolled down.

They skirted a marble tank of water and crossed the courtyard, still littered with golden straw and silver fish scales. Feral cats were feeding on discarded fish-heads and cracked lobster claws. They scattered as the friends approached.

'Hello?' called Flavia as they reached the half-opened doorway of the shop. 'Anybody here?'

'Anybody here?' squawked Siptax from the cage in Jonathan's hand.

'We're closed.' A fat woman with a twig broom appeared at the doorway. A tiny monkey in a red tunic perched on her shoulder.

'Do you have any oysters left?' asked Flavia.

'Afraid not,' said the woman, 'Come back tomorrow.'

'Hey!' cried Jonathan as the monkey leapt onto his shoulder.

'Trimalchio!' said the woman sternly. 'Leave him alone!'

The monkey ignored her and began to search for ticks in Jonathan's hair. Jonathan laughed as he felt the deft little fingers rapidly parting his curls. 'You won't find much up there,' he said to the monkey. 'I hope.'

'Oh, he's the most adorable thing I've ever seen!' cried Flavia. 'Look at his little red tunic and his dear little face – oh!' The monkey had abandoned Jonathan and was now examining Flavia's hair. Expertly he removed one hairpin after another and tossed them onto the marble courtyard.

'Trimalchio!' said the woman with a scowl. 'Come away at once! Bad Trimalchio!'

'Trimalchio!' squawked the bird. 'Bad Trimalchio!'

'Why do you call him Trimalchio?' asked Jonathan.

The woman shrugged. 'Wasn't me that named him, and it certainly wasn't me that bought him. In fact, I wish I'd never seen him,' said the woman with a scowl, as Trimalchio leapt from Flavia to Nubia. He put his little arms around her neck and gave her a monkey-kiss.

They all laughed as he turned to give them a mischievous look of bright intelligence, before jumping back into his mistress's plump arms.

'Now that,' said Flavia as they walked slowly home, 'that would have been the perfect pet for Lupus.'

COME TO A PARTY
CELEBRATING YOUR NINTH BIRTHDAY
TODAY AT THE NINTH HOUR
THERE'LL BE NINE OYSTERS FOR YOU
AND QUAILS' EGGS, TOO,
LETTUCE AND LOVAGE,
AND PARTRIDGE PIE
WITH WILD MUSHROOMS AND ONIONS
(COOKED BY JONATHAN)
PRESENTS, GARLANDS, MUSIC,
WELL–WATERED WINE
AND BEST OF ALL
NINE FRIENDS: SIX OLD AND THREE NEW.

'Happy Birthday!' cried Flavia and Nubia together, as Lupus stepped into the atrium. Jonathan followed. He held his barbiton in one hand. It was the third hour after noon on the Kalends of February.

Lupus's dark hair was clean and perfumed with jasmine-scented oil. He wore a new long-sleeved white tunic and a sea-green hooded cloak. On his feet were fox-fur lined boots and around his waist a leather belt which also served as a sling.

As they entered the triclinium Flavia handed out

fragrant garlands of winter jasmine. Scuto, Tigris and Nipur were waiting for them with wagging tails and jasmine garlands entwined in their collars.

'I promised you six old friends,' said Flavia. 'Here we are: three people and three dogs!'

Lupus grinned as the three dogs licked him and barked their birthday greetings. Then he gazed around the triclinium. A dozen hanging oil-lamps shone like golden stars against the red-frescoed panels depicting the exploits of Hercules. Draped between each of the lamp-holders were smiling curves of green ivy twined with creamy winter jasmine.

'You'll meet your three new friends in a minute,' said Flavia. 'But first, let's have some quails' eggs and oysters. Take the central couch,' she added, 'the place of honour.'

'You can have my oysters,' said Jonathan, climbing onto the right-hand couch. 'They're so fresh they're still alive.'

'Later,' said Flavia, 'we're going to have some of Jonathan's famous partridge pie! But first we are going to perform you a birthday song!'

She and Nubia perched on the left-hand couch. Nubia pulled out her cherry-wood flute and on the couch opposite, Jonathan strummed his barbiton. Then Flavia began to sing.

ODE TO LUPUS

I sing of Lupus the Greek, a hero of Titus's reign,
Help me Muse, inspire me as I sing of Lupus the wolf.
He came from bright isles in the wine-dark Aegean
One day he tried to avert a crime, a terrible injustice,
a crime which made even the Furies gasp in horror.
But for his bravery he was punished, punished
with the loss of his tongue –
O terrible to tell – denied speech itself.

He was imprisoned in the dark belly of a wasp:
Vespa, in the fetid hull of the slave-dealer's ship,
his enemy's vessel.
But one day on the far, fair shores of Ostia, near
the river mouth chosen by Aeneas himself
Fortuna met with him, gracious and kind,
her head garlanded with justice,
and she whispered words of encouragement.
Then did Lupus escape the clutches of his enemy,
a Cyclops with one eye and an appetite for evil.
Disguised as a beggar, like Odysseus of old,
our young hero lived among the tombs.
At first the pain and grief of all that he had endured
made him want to lick his wounds, like an injured beast.
But soon he learned to beg and sometimes steal
– because even heroes steal sometimes –
until one day a pack of slavering dogs
chased Lupus through the scented pines.

Like a lone wolf he fled
from the pack who would tear him.
He could not go right, nor could he go left;
Upwards was his only recourse, his only road above.
So up he went, up a lofty umbrella pine.
Then, like Icarus, he fell from the sky,
not onto billowing waves, his native element,
but onto hard earth,
which jars the bones and bruises the flesh.
For wolves may swim and wolves may run,
but never do wolves fly in the air.
Lupus fell out of that tree into our lives
and we thank you, Fortuna,
because you sometimes show surprising mercy
and what seems like disaster is really a blessing!
Thank you, Fair Fortuna, for bringing us this wolf,
for bringing us our Lupus!

Lupus grinned and clapped enthusiastically as the song ended.

'Now,' said Flavia, flushed with pleasure at the success of her ode. 'It's time to meet your three new friends!'

Lupus sat up on his couch as Flavia, Jonathan and Nubia put down their instruments and left the dining room. A few moments later they returned, each holding a cage. Nubia's was tiny, Jonathan's medium, and Flavia's large.

Nubia put her tiny wooden cage on the couch beside Lupus.

Inside was a beautiful beetle, like a shimmering green emerald.

'It is Egyptian scarab beetle,' said Nubia softly. 'Is very lucky.' She gave him a quick kiss on the cheek. 'Happy Birthday, Lupus.'

'Happy Birthday, Lupus!' squawked the occupant of the medium-sized cage, and Lupus nearly tumbled off the couch.

'Euge!' cried Flavia. 'He did it!'

'Siptax,' said Jonathan, setting the wicker cage beside Lupus, 'is a talking bird and I am not going to kiss you.' He grinned. 'Happy Birthday, Lupus!'

'And this,' Flavia stepped forward dramatically with a bamboo cage, 'is Trimalchio the monkey!'

Lupus opened the little door and gave a bark of laughter as the monkey swarmed out of his cage and up the sleeve of his white birthday tunic. Trimalchio brought his wrinkled little face close to Lupus's for a moment, and Flavia smiled. Early that morning, when they had gone back for oysters, the woman had agreed to let them have the monkey for only twenty sesterces – cage included – a fabulous bargain.

The monkey's movements were quick and precise as he searched for ticks in Lupus's hair. Not finding any there, he jumped back down onto the couch. The dogs stopped gnawing their bones and gazed up at the monkey with interest. Trimalchio bounced over to one of the small tables and devoured the last three quail's eggs on the plate.

'Hey!' laughed Flavia. 'You've already had your dinner, Trimalchio!'

The monkey ignored her and began on Jonathan's oysters, deftly tipping them into his mouth and throwing the shells at the dogs, who retreated back under their couches.

Lupus lunged for Trimalchio, but the monkey leapt up to one of the half dozen bronze lamp-holders fixed into the frescoed wall. Oil-lamps hung on chains attached to these horizontal rods, and garlands were draped between them. As Trimalchio hopped up and down on one of the bronze rods, the flickering lamp beneath it began to swing alarmingly.

'Come down, Trimalchio!' commanded Flavia. 'You'll set the house on fire!'

'Yes, Trimalchio! Come here!' said Jonathan. 'Bad monkey!'

'Bad monkey!' scolded Siptax. 'Bad monkey!'

Trimalchio looked down at them with his intelligent little eyes and made a chattering noise which sounded like laughter. Then – quick as lightning – he leapt to another lamp-holder, then down onto Nubia's head and across to Siptax's cage. Gripping the wicker bars with his tiny black hands he gave the cage such a violent shake that Siptax fell off his perch.

'Long live Caesar!' screeched the bird, flapping about his cage. 'Long live Caesar!'

Trimalchio threw down the cage and it knocked over the ceramic jug of wine. The wine jar and bird cage both shattered on the floor of the triclinium. Released from his confinement, Siptax fluttered wildly around the dining room, decorating the floor with his droppings and screaming: 'Long live Caesar!' The dogs ran to the wine and began lapping it up.

Flavia squealed and covered her head while Nubia and the boys clambered over the couches trying to catch Trimalchio.

But the monkey was out of control. Chattering mischievously, he snatched something from the couch and retreated to the safety of a lofty lamp-holder. The bronze lamp swung wildly on its chain, spilling drops of hot oil on the couch below.

Flavia cautiously uncovered her head and looked around. 'Is the bird gone?' I'm afraid he'll get tangled in my hair.'

Her three friends did not reply. They stood on the left-hand couch, gazing up at the central wall. Flavia followed their gaze.

The oil-lamp had stopped swinging. Trimalchio sat quietly on the lamp-holder, examining a tiny wooden cage.

'What's he got?' cried Flavia. And then, 'Oh, no!'

'It is lucky scarab!' said Nubia.

'Oh dear,' said Jonathan, as Trimalchio opened the cage door and took out the beetle. 'He's not very lucky anymore.'

Nubia leapt onto the central couch, but she was too late. Trimalchio had popped the emerald dung-beetle into his mouth and was munching it with gusto.

'Alas!' wailed Nubia. 'He is eating the lucky scarab!'

As Trimalchio happily devoured the beetle, the dogs barked drunkenly. Then, with a final cry of 'Long live Caesar!' Siptax flew out of the wide triclinium doorway. With a chitter of excitement Trimalchio swarmed after him.

Lupus, Flavia, Jonathan and Nubia scrambled off their couches and ran to the doorway of the triclinium, just in time to see the monkey swing from the upper branches of the fig tree to the inner balcony and from there up to the terracotta roof tiles and onto the top of the town wall. For a moment he looked down at them. Then he was gone.

The four friends turned and stared at the dining room. The wine jug lay in pieces on the floor, along with oyster shells, a broken cage and a decorative pattern of white bird droppings. The three dogs were staggering from couch to couch with silly grins on their faces.

Jonathan slowly bent and rose again. He held a bright green feather between his forefinger and thumb. Suddenly he started.

'Oh, Pollux!' he cried, and ran out of the triclinium. A moment later he was back, using a thick cloth to hold something which resembled a blackened discus. 'This,' he said miserably, 'is my famous partridge pie with onion, walnut and wild mushrooms. It's burnt to a cinder.'

Back on his couch Lupus sat hunched over, his shoulders shaking.

'Oh, Lupus,' said Flavia. 'Please don't cry.'

'We just wanted to give you good birthday.' whispered Nubia.

'I'm sorry the food is burnt,' said Jonathan miserably.

Lupus looked up, laughing. He took out his wax tablet and they all moved closer to read what he was writing:

I DON'T MIND. CAN'T TASTE IT ANYWAY.
THANK YOU FOR THE PARTY.
IT'S THE BEST ONE I'VE EVER BEEN TO!

— AUTHOR'S NOTE —

Fans often ask, 'Why doesn't Lupus have a pet?' After all, Flavia, Jonathan and Nubia all have dogs. That gave me the idea of writing a short story about how Lupus's three friends want to give him a pet. This story also solves the mystery of when he was born.

JONATHAN
VS. IRA

This short story takes place in March AD 80,
between book VII, *The Enemies of Jupiter*, and
book VIII, *The Gladiators from Capua*.

DAY I

I am dead.

Or rather the person I used to be is dead.

Jonathan ben Mordecai. Born in Jerusalem during the last year of Nero's reign. Moved to Italia after the Romans destroyed Jerusalem. Lived in Rome, then Ostia.

When Jonathan was eleven he went to Rome to try to do a good thing. But instead of doing something good he did something so terrible that afterwards he wanted to kill himself.

But he was a coward. Not brave enough to kill himself.

Instead, he signed up to be a gladiator. He told himself that death was too quick. He told himself that he should 'atone for his crime' – like Hercules. But really Jonathan was just a big coward. He was afraid to throw himself off the cliff.

Everybody knows you have to be at least twenty-five to sign up as a gladiator. But that's only if you're freeborn. The Emperor needs lots of performers for the inaugural games at his new amphitheatre. Even slaves and criminals. No questions asked. You could win fame, gold, even freedom. Lots of slaves have signed up, some of them kids, like me. They're training the children to be the novelty act. We'll be fighting and dying after the noon executions, while Senators go to Titus's new baths, and poor people eat picnic lunches in their seats.

When Jonathan pretended to be a slave and signed up to be a gladiator he made one mistake. He chose a new name for himself.

Names are powerful. When you know someone's name you have power over them. That is why we Jews never speak God's name.

When Jonathan told the scribe his new name – his arena name – he suddenly realised that a new part of him had come into existence.

He felt different.

And he realised he could have more than one name for himself.

So when he came here to the gladiator school, he didn't tell anyone his real name or his arena name. He chose a third name. The name I have now.

Ira.

It means 'anger' in Latin.

I like it.

One or two of them found out about my old name but I never answer. Soon nobody will call me Jonathan. Everybody will call me Ira.

Jonathan wanted to suffer. I have other plans. Now that I am a gladiator I'm going to become tough. Jonathan had asthma. I discovered that when I get angry the asthma goes away. Also, when I feel anger it covers up the pain inside. Therefore anger is good. That's why my new name is Ira.

DAY II

One of the other boys tried to be nice to me today. He asked me if I wanted to 'talk about it'. Apparently Jonathan was crying in his sleep. Macedo has hair the colour of dirty sand and big lips like a girl's. When he asked me if I wanted to 'talk about it' I punched him hard, right in his girl's mouth. Now he leaves me alone. Today was our first proper day of training. I'm exhausted but I'm going to write down as much as I can. After breakfast – disgusting barley porridge – they took us out to inspect us. We are staying in the Golden House. It was built by Nero. After he died they didn't know what to do with it. Finally, because a fire burnt the old quarters and because this place is near the new amphitheatre, they moved us gladiators here. We sleep ten to a room.

The rooms are huge and vaulted, with frescoes on the walls. But our cots are rock hard.

They spread sand over a grassy courtyard to make a practice arena. When the trumpet blows we all have to run out there and stand barefoot on the sand.

The lanista – the head trainer – is called Rotundus. He made us all strip down to our loincloths. Some people laughed at me because I have some blubber around the middle. I noted who they were and stored up my anger.

Rotundus sorted us into different groups. He sent some to be murmillos or secutors. The skinny ones will be net-men, retiarii. They're the lowest of the low. They don't even get helmets and you can see their faces. All they do is run away, said our trainer Spartacus.

He's training us to be hoplomachi and Thracians. A Thracian – Thraex – is a type of gladiator who fights with a curved sword and a small square shield called a parma. Hoplomachi are just Thracians with round shields and no griffins on their helmets. Our trainer is named after the most famous Thraex. Spartacus told us that even the Emperor Titus supports us Thracians, because we are the best.

Spartacus gave us wooden practice swords and started us out on some simple training exercises. Swing right, parry, swing left, parry. Soon my arm was on fire. We had to lunge forward too, and I suppose that's why my side and thighs ache today. At noon we had more barley porridge, this time with beans.

'Better get used to it,' said Cook, when people complained. 'That's why they call gladiators "barley eaters".'

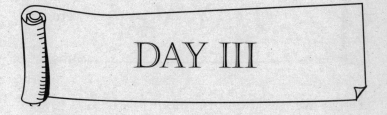

DAY III

We trained for six hours solid this morning. We started by running three times around the hill. Then exercises. Already by mid-morning the muscles in my arms were screaming. This time we are hitting big wooden posts.

After our usual barley lunch we went to the baths. We soaked in the hot plunge for a while and then were told to attend the adult gladiators in our group. Some of the bath-slaves showed us how to give a rubdown. I hated that. The man I was massaging had a hairy back. It was steamy and I started to wheeze. Then I remembered.

I wasn't Jonathan anymore.

I was Ira.

I let the anger fill me as I pummelled his disgusting back. My lungs eased and I could breathe again. Later, Hairy-back said: 'That was the best massage I've had in a long time.' And he tossed me a denarius.

DAY VII

Today we tried on our armour for the first time. I wear padding on my legs, and over that tall bronze greaves – leg-guards – which make me walk with stiff legs. But I don't mind. It makes me feel different. I have a manica – a padded arm guard – and a shield: blood red with four palm branches for victory painted on each corner. The helmet is beautiful and frightening at the same time. It has a griffin head on the crest and the disc gratings on the visor look like a fly's eyes. When I put it on everything changes.

I can hear myself breathing and my own heart beating. I smell the sweaty linen padding and the animal fat they use to polish it. I only see my opponent through the visor. Wearing my helmet makes me feel strong and protected. It makes me feel like Ira.

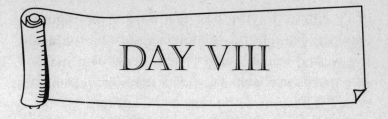

DAY VIII

Today we trained wearing our armour again.

The first thing Spartacus taught us was the famous Thracian 'At Ease' position. You bend the left leg slightly and rest the shield on your greave, holding your sword loosely in your right hand. Next he taught us the 'Attack' position: you crouch with left leg forward, bringing your shield up to your visor. The front of your shield and your left greave should make a straight line. Your sword arm is back and ready.

Jonathan used to have a clay oil-lamp with a Thracian in attack pose. Now I am that Thracian.

DAY XII

I just smashed my fist into the wall.

That was stupid.

Someone took the sheets of papyrus with my

diary entries for the past few days. I lost control. Now my hand hurts, my knuckles are bleeding and I've wasted valuable anger. Whoever took the pieces of papyrus probably can't even read. He'll probably wipe his bottom with them at the latrines.

Never mind. I'll find a better hiding place for my writing things. And I can say in one word what the missing pages said: TRAINED.

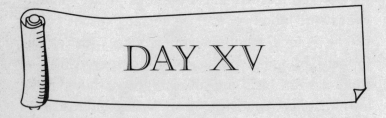

DAY XV

Nobody stole my pages this time. There's just nothing new to say.

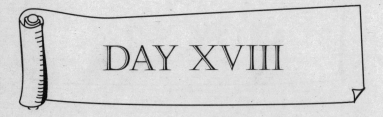

DAY XVIII

My day is like this.

I get up at dawn. I use the pot in the corner. A

bowl of barley porridge at the long table in the mess room.

Hitting a post for three hours. A break if we're lucky.

After the break we spar with each other. At noon we have lunch: more barley porridge. Then some exercise at the baths. Sometimes I give a massage. Sometimes I get one. After a short nap, we polish our helmets and armour. Sometimes we have lectures on technique. Maybe a chance to pick nits out of our hair.

About an hour before dusk we eat dinner, usually meat and beans. They blow the trumpet at lamp-lighting time. That's the signal for bed. I sleep like a statue. I barely put my head on the straw-filled mattress before the trumpet blares us out of bed again.

DAY XX

I was training with Spartacus today, armour but no helmets. I was using my anger, fighting well. Or so I thought.

Suddenly I was on my back, the wind knocked out

of me and his sword – real not wooden – inches from my face. 'Never think how well you're doing,' he said. 'Otherwise you'll end up underneath . . . like this. And wipe that look off your face. You've made yourself hard. That's fine. You've learned to channel your anger. Even better. But a good gladiator never betrays what he is feeling. Even when you wear a helmet your face must never show anger. Or surprise. Or fear. Or pain.'

Then he touched my chin with the tip of his sword and flicked.

It hurt like Hades but I didn't cry out.

'Good,' he said. 'Much better. You hardly flinched at all. Now go mop up the blood and apply some styptic. Then come back and we'll continue.'

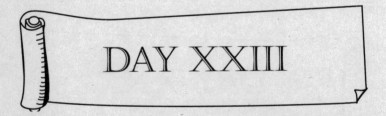

DAY XXIII

Only three days until we fight in the new amphitheatre. They say it takes six months of constant training just to become a tiro, a novice. I've been here less than four weeks. In so many ways I'm nowhere near ready. But in one way, I am ready.

Nobody has called me Jonathan for a long time. These days they only ever call me Ira.

— AUTHOR'S NOTE —

I wanted to write about how a gladiator is trained. What they eat, what they do, where they sleep. But I didn't want Jonathan to appear in *The Gladiators from Capua* until about a third of the way in. So I decided to write this short story. Also, I thought I would try out writing in first person, i.e. getting into Jonathan's head. The mystery is: What was the terrible thing Jonathan did? (Read *The Enemies of Jupiter* to find out.)

THE CASE
OF THE CITRUS-
WOOD TABLE

This short story takes place in April AD 80,
between book VIII, *The Gladiators from Capua*,
and book IX, *The Colossus of Rhodes*.

'This is it: the scene of the crime!'

Flavia Gemina, a highborn Roman girl, stood in the sunny inner garden of a small Ostian townhouse and looked at her three friends. 'Faber says he can only give us one hour to investigate; then his guests start arriving for dinner.'

'What was stolen?' asked Jonathan ben Mordecai. 'A table?'

'Not just any table,' said Flavia. 'A valuable citrus-wood table.'

'A table is valuable?' said a pretty dark-skinned girl with a frown. Nubia was Flavia's former slave-girl. She had only been in Italia for a year and did not always understand Roman ways.

'This one is,' said Flavia. 'It's worth half a million sesterces.'

A dark-haired boy in a sea-green tunic gave Flavia a bug-eyed look.

'That's right, Lupus. Half a million sesterces.'

Lupus opened his wax tablet. Using his bronze stylus, he scratched a message in the thin layer of beeswax that coated one of the wooden leaves:

YOU COULD BUY A SHIP FOR THAT

Flavia nodded grimly. 'Two weeks ago Argentarius the banker accidentally knocked over his wife's favourite table. He brought it here to his friend

Faber the carpenter and asked him to repair it. They had no idea it was so valuable. Argentarius thought it was just a little round table with three bronze legs, but when his wife got back from Rome yesterday and found it missing, she went berserk. She threatened to toss him in the Tiber if he didn't bring it straight back.' Flavia consulted her own wax tablet. 'Faber says he put it in the storeroom intending to repair it. But when Argentarius came to collect it today, it was gone. There were no signs of a break-in, but Faber remembers when he got back from the forum last week the front door was ajar. Nothing seemed to be missing then, and he didn't think to check the storeroom. The clues may be up to a week old,' she snapped her wax tablet shut, 'but it's up to us to find them. Argentarius has promised us a gold coin each if we can solve the mystery.'

'What sort of clues should we look for?' asked Jonathan.

'Well,' said Flavia, gesturing to the deep red panels on the walls of the peristyle, 'Faber says these frescoes are brand new. So look for greasy hand prints.'

Lupus raised his eyebrows at Flavia.

'If there's a greasy hand print,' explained Flavia, 'that shows us the crime was committed at night because the culprit must have been holding an oil-lamp. Furthermore, it proves the thief was a poor person. If they were rich they'd be holding a bronze oil-lamp, not a cheap clay one that sweats oil and makes your hand greasy!'

'What else?' said Jonathan.

'According to Faber, the black-and-white mosaic of the guard dog in the vestibule is also brand new,' said Flavia. 'See if there are any tesserae missing. Tesserae are the little marble chips,' she reminded Nubia. 'If one is missing it might have got stuck to the bottom of the thief's boot or sandal.'

'So all we have to do,' remarked Jonathan drily, 'is search the shoe-soles of everybody here in Ostia.'

'Exactly,' said Flavia brightly, 'And speaking of shoe-soles, look for any footprints in the garden. Most outdoor shoes have hobnails on the bottom and each pattern is slightly different. If any of you find a shoe-print, call Lupus. He's the best at drawing so he can copy the pattern onto his wax tablet. Faber said he's just had new turf put in so the soil should still be moist and fresh.'

'Um . . . Flavia?' said Jonathan, raising his hand.

'What is it, Jonathan?' said Flavia with a sigh, glancing at the new sundial in the centre of the freshly-planted garden, 'We don't have much time.'

'Don't you think it's a bit strange that in the past two weeks Faber has had a new mosaic laid, freshly-plastered walls and a brand new garden installed with a bronze-and-marble sundial as its outstanding feature?'

Flavia stared at him blankly.

'I'll wager,' said Jonathan, 'that Faber realised the value of the table, sold it and has been using his profits to redecorate.'

'Great Jupiter's eyebrows!' exclaimed Flavia. 'You're right. Faber probably reckoned that as Argentarius didn't know the true worth of the table, he could fob him off with one that looked nicer but was worth much less. I was so busy looking at each little clue, I didn't see the mosaic for the tesserae! Euge, Jonathan! I think you've just solved the case of the citrus-wood table!'

— AUTHOR'S NOTE —

I often play with my replica Roman artefacts and think how they could be clues to a crime. One day I bought a replica clay oil-lamp from a museum shop. When I got it home I filled it with olive oil, put in a piece of twine for a wick, and lit it. It worked! After a while it started to get dark outside. Instead of turning on the lights, I took the oil-lamp and explored my flat, pretending I was Flavia looking for clues. After a while, I noticed my hand was sticky from the oil which had been sweating through the porous clay of the lamp. This gave me the idea for the clue of the greasy handprint. Not long after this, I was reading the part of Pliny's *Natural History* where he talks about tables made of citrus wood. These were fabulously expensive and desirable. So 'The Case of the Citrus-wood Table' was born.

THE CASE OF THE TALKING STATUE

This short story takes place in October AD 80, between book XII, *The Charioteer of Delphi,* and, book XIII, *The Slave-girl from Jerusalem.*

'It's a prodigy!' A plump Roman woman of about thirty threw open the front door so violently that she almost crushed the door-slave who had unbolted it. 'A prodigy!' she repeated, bustling into the atrium.

'Alma!' cried eleven-year-old Flavia Gemina. 'What is it? What's happened?' Flavia and her three friends all stood up. They had been having lessons with their young Greek tutor Aristo. He rose, too, and from beneath the table emerged three barking dogs, excited by this sudden activity.

'A talking statue!' Alma had to shout to make herself heard above the dogs. 'Cult statue in the little temple of Spes near the theatre!' Alma set down her baskets full of fruit and vegetables, and pressed a hand to her chest. 'Oh dear!' she gasped.

'Sit down, Alma. Catch your breath.' Flavia turned to the door-slave. 'Caudex, fetch her a beaker of posca. Quickly!'

'Right away,' mumbled Caudex, and shuffled out of the atrium towards the kitchen.

Aristo pulled back his chair for Alma, who sat and fanned herself with her hand. Flavia looked at her ex-nursemaid with fond concern; Alma was as dear to her as the mother she had lost when she was three years old.

'Which one is temple of Spes?' Nubia looked up from calming the dogs.

'Isn't it one of the four small temples near the

theatre?' said Flavia's next-door neighbour Jonathan. 'Not that I've been inside, of course. Being Jewish and all.'

'Oh, I know!' cried Flavia. 'Nubia, you remember! It's near the little Temple of Saturn! That was where you captured the escaped lion durning the Saturnalia last year!'

'Correct,' said Aristo. 'The Temple of Spes is located at the end of a row of the four small temples near the theatre. It's next to the temples of Venus, Saturn and Fortuna. Spes is the personification of Hope,' he added, for Nubia's benefit: 'That is, the abstract concept of hope represented as a young girl on the verge of marriage.'

The youngest of them – a boy with green eyes and brown hair – minced forward, swinging his hips and holding up imaginary skirts with his left hand. In his right hand he pretended to hold something and then delicately sniff it. Lupus could not speak, and for this reason he often acted out what he wanted to say.

Caudex had just returned to the atrium. He stared at Lupus with a puzzled expression, then handed a beaker to Alma.

'Lupus is right,' said Flavia. 'The cult statue of Spes is a girl holding the hem of her stola in one hand and a flower in the other.' Flavia turned to Alma. 'Is that the statue that spoke?'

Alma nodded over the rim of her beaker. When

she had drained it, she plunked down the cup, wiped her mouth with the back of her plump hand, and looked round at their attentive faces, clearly relishing every moment of their attention.

'Tell us, Alma!' cried Flavia. 'What did the statue say?'

Alma leaned forward and lowered her voice to a dramatic whisper. 'The statue said: *Hope will blossom when Ostia picks the crocus*. And she didn't say it just one or twice, but thrice!'

'*Hope will blossom when Ostia picks the crocus,*' repeated Flavia, and then: 'Alma, are you sure that's what the statue said?'

Alma nodded firmly. 'Heard it myself with these two ears.'

'What did statue voice sound like?' asked Nubia.

'Like a little girl,' said Alma. 'But clear like. There was no mistaking it.'

'No,' said Jonathan, folding his arms across his chest and shaking his head. 'I'm sorry, but I don't believe it. Statues don't talk. It's a trick.'

Lupus pointed at Jonathan and nodded, as if to say: I agree with him.

'But I heard it myself,' said Alma.

'I believe you,' said Flavia.

'Were there any other witnesses?' said Jonathan.

'A dozen, at least!' said Alma. 'You see, I was visiting

the little Temple of Venus with my friend Rustica because there's this good-looking new door-slave at her house, and she wanted to make an offering for . . . well, you know. Anyway, we were just leaving when there was a commotion at one of the other little temples and we went to see what it was about, and there were about ten or twelve people there – mostly women – and one of them said to be quiet because she might speak again, and we said who and she said the cult statue and that she'd spoken twice already, and we was all quiet and sure enough the statue said "Hope will blossom when Ostia picks the Crocus." I heard it as clear as you can hear me. Then some of them yelled and others shushed the yelling ones, but most was saying how it was a prodigy and some of them have gone to fetch the aedile.'

'Ideal?' said Nubia.

'The aedile,' said Aristo, 'is one of Ostia's junior magistrates. His job includes investigating portents.'

'I think we should investigate, too,' said Flavia, 'To solve the mystery.'

'What mystery?' said Jonathan. 'You just said you believed Alma.'

'I believe she heard something. But was it really the statue speaking, or a hoax? And if it was really the statue, what does the cryptic message mean?'

'And if it was a hoax,' said Jonathan, 'what does the cryptic message mean?'

'Yes!' cried Flavia, and looked at her tutor. 'May we investigate, Aristo? Please?'

Aristo looked round at their eager faces. It was still two hours before noon. 'If you can give me,' he said, 'a literary or historical reference to something like this happening before, then I'll let you go and investigate.'

'A reference to something like what?' asked Jonathan.

'Statues speaking. Or sweating,' added Aristo. 'Turning round. Falling down.'

Jonathan raised an eyebrow. 'This happens a lot? Statues talking and spinning around? So much that they need a special magistrate to investigate?'

'Don't be silly, Jonathan,' said Flavia. 'Of course it doesn't happen a lot. That's why it's an omen.'

'Prodigy,' said Aristo. 'Technically it's a prodigy. An omen is personal. A prodigy is social. For the whole community. The statue mentioned Ostia, so in this case it's a prodigy.' He smiled at her. 'So, no reference? I can think of three or four.'

'Oh, tell us Aristo!' cried Flavia.

'No. I want you to tell me.'

Nubia shyly raised her hand. 'There is sweaty statue of Athena in the *Aeneid* of Virgil.'

'Nubia, you're right!' cried Flavia. 'After the Greeks steal the Palladium from the Trojans, lightning flashes from her eyes and salty sweat bathes her limbs.'

Lupus gave the girls his bug-eyed look of amazement, and they all laughed. A moment later they all cheered as Aristo rolled up his papyrus scroll.

'Well done,' he said with a grin. 'You may go and investigate the prodigy.'

Just past Ostia's theatre, on the way to the port, was a narrow side street leading behind a nymphaeum and into an enclosed square with shops, a fountain and four small temples. When Flavia and her friends arrived, the area around the nymphaeum was so jammed with people that they overflowed back onto the Decumanus Maximus. The fan-shaped crowd of people were trying to shuffle forward, but without success.

Someone on the other side of the crowd must have been pushing because suddenly the people directly in front of them began to surge backwards. A matron with a papyrus parasol trod on Flavia's foot.

'Pollux!' she cursed. 'It's too crowded here. We'll never get in this way.' She turned. 'Lupus, you know Ostia like the back of your hand. Is there another way to get in to that little square?'

Lupus shrugged and glanced around. Flavia saw his head go back as his gaze travelled up the curved outer wall of the theatre, looming above them. He grinned and beckoned them to follow.

They turned and pushed through the growing

crowd and a few moments later they were following Lupus through the theatre's vaulted entrance. As they emerged into the vast curved space of the seating – the cavea – Flavia saw that it was completely empty. There were no awnings, and the morning sun sparkled brightly on the gleaming marble seats. Lupus began to climb the stairs to the top, taking an aisle that would lead them to the western end of the cavea.

'Oh, I know what he's doing!' cried Flavia, as she puffed after Lupus.

At last, breathing hard from the climb, the four friends reached the highest row of the theatre. Lupus stood on the marble seat and looked over the wall. Flavia joined him, her heart thudding from the climb. All Ostia lay before her, and directly below was the Square of the Four Temples.

'Great Juno's peacock!' she breathed. 'It's packed down there. She glanced over at Nubia and Jonathan, who had stepped up beside her.

'Look,' wheezed Jonathan, pointing. 'See that narrow alley . . . behind the four temples? Someone could hide back there . . . and speak through a doorway.' He paused to catch his breath. 'Or they could whisper through a hole in the back wall . . . right behind the statue. It would seem as if the statue had spoken. If they used a speaking tube . . . they could even magnify their voice.'

Flavia nodded. 'I'm glad we're not down there. Those people are getting squashed.'

'They look like sheeps in a fold,' observed Nubia and Lupus grunted his agreement.

There was the sound of a splash. Lupus guffawed and pointed down.

'Oops!' giggled Flavia. 'Somebody has fallen into the nymphaeum.'

'THE STATUE OF SPES HAS SPOKEN!' came a voice from the direction of the forum. It was Praeco, the town crier. 'CLEAR THE WAY SO THE AEDILE CAN INVESTIGATE!'

Now they could hear rumblings of panic rising up from the temple precinct below, then the sudden shriek of a woman or eunuch. Lupus grunted and pointed to the crowd of people on the other side of the shops, those still trying to get in. As they watched, a young man in a flapping toga appeared. He was preceded by Praeco the town crier and two lictors; behind him clumped a phalanx of twenty vigiles. The togaed man was obviously some kind of official because he began barking orders and pointing.

'Is that the ideal?' said Nubia.

'Aedile,' Flavia corrected, and added. 'I'm not sure. I don't think aediles have lictors.'

'Lick doors?' asked Nubia with a frown.

'Those men with iron rods,' explained Jonathan. 'They act as bodyguards and they usually accompany the duovirs or praetors. Maybe he borrowed some.'

Following the magistrate's instructions, the vigiles quickly ushered people out of the dangerously packed temple precinct. Soon they had formed the crowd into an excited but orderly queue. This line of people now extended from the temple of Spes across the precinct, through the corridor between the shops and along the Decumanus Maximus towards the forum.

'That's better,' said Jonathan. 'And nobody seems to have been hurt.'

'We'd better join the queue,' sighed Flavia, 'but it will be hours now before we get to the temple.'

A sudden noise came from the theatre behind them: the crunch of hobnail boots on the marble stage.

'Behold!' cried Nubia, 'Soldiers arrest them.'

They all turned to see two vigiles ushering people out onto the stage of the theatre and down some steps towards the exit.

'They must have been disorderly,' said Jonathan.
'I don't think they're prisoners,' said Flavia. 'Those soldiers seem to be guiding them, not guarding them. They're probably bringing them this way to keep the flow of people moving and avoid another crush.' Flavia's grey eyes widen. 'That means there's another way out . . . and another way in!'

'They won't let us in down there,' said Jonathan. He turned and pointed back down to the square below. 'Look. They've got the people all organized.' See how the line goes in one side of the temple and comes out the other? And then comes out this back entrance? The vigiles might let us get *out* this way, but they'll never let us *in*.'

'I'll bet Lupus could find a way in, couldn't you?' said Flavia. 'Lupus? Lupus?' She looked around and then grinned at the others. 'What did I tell you?'

Lupus allowed himself a smile of satisfaction as he slipped through the theatre door and down the steps past the queue of chattering Ostians. From their conversation he gathered the statue had not spoken again, but people were excited anyway.

'She smiled at me,' said one woman.

'Me, too,' said another.

'She looked sad to me,' said a dwarf.

Lupus snorted. How could a statue smile, or look sad, or speak? He was certain it was a trick and he intended to prove it.

Once down the steps, Lupus walked casually toward the back of the Temple of Spes. There was a dark, narrow alley back here. A guard was looking in his direction, so he turned and pretended to do his business against the wall. As soon as the guard looked away, Lupus slipped into the alley. It smelt of urine – and worse – so he went carefully.

The sudden beat of wings made him freeze, but it

was only a few startled pigeons. The stone walls of the alley magnified the sound of their wings and presently their throaty cooing. Lupus remembered what Jonathan had said about someone using a speaking tube through the back wall of the temple. But there were no windows or holes or even cracks in the thick rear wall.

However, one of the two middle temples had a back door with three steps leading down.

At the foot of these steps was a pile of used candles, rotted fruit and withered garlands: old offerings tossed out by the priest. Lupus went up the steps and examined the door. Solid oak and no handle or even keyhole on this side. He tried pushing but it was solid as rock and his hand came away dusty. There were no other marks on the outside of the door, only his, and no fresh footprints that he could see. From this he deduced that he was the first person to come this way for some time.

That meant they could rule out one method of entry, as well as Jonathan's theory of how a statue might speak. Lupus stepped over the temple rubbish and went all the way down the alley, just to confirm there was no other way in or out.

There wasn't.

Treading carefully, he made his way back to the line of people emerging from the temple. He pretended to be lost and looking for someone.

Presently he saw a matron with two girls and squeezed into the line behind them. A bony finger tapped him on the shoulder and he turned to see an old woman scowling at him. Lupus recognized her as Hariola, an Egyptian fortune-teller who had a tiny room up on Ropemakers Street.

'You pushed in front of me,' she rasped. She stank of cheap musk oil.

Lupus shook his head and pointed wide-eyed at the matron in front of him.

'She's not your mother,' snorted Hariola. 'You're an orphan. You're that tongueless boy who used to beg for coppers in the Medusa Tavern.'

Lupus shrugged, turned away from her and kept his head down. Luckily they were just entering the Temple of Spes.

'Move along,' said a bored guard with a yawn. He was leaning against one of the polished marble columns. 'Lay your offerings and move along.'

As they moved from the bright light of a hot October morning into the cool dimness of the temple, the chattering crowd grew silent. It smelt faintly of incense and saffron. Before the cult statue was a little heap of crocuses. Even as Lupus watched, the matron and her two little girls reverently placed their own purple blooms on the growing pile. To the right of the cult statue was the aedile. He sat on a folding chair, and behind him

76

stood a scribe with a wax tablet and stylus, poised and ready. They both stared attentively at the cult statue of Spes.

Lupus followed their gaze. He had seen the statue before and it looked as it always did: a painted marble sculpture of a girl stepping forward with a flower in her right hand and a look of expectancy on her face. She stood on a low plinth of green marble, and he could see immediately that there was no place for a trickster to crouch behind it.

But the culprit had to be hiding somewhere. If he was to discover how the trick had been performed he needed to find a place to hide, too, so that he could wait and watch unseen. He glanced around the little cella. Up above were four wooden beams from which oil-lamps hung. The right hand and back walls were solid. So was the floor. However, an open doorway pierced the left hand wall; presumably it led to the little temple of Fortuna. Yes! He could spy from in there.

But he needed a distraction, something to catch people's attention so he could slip next door and keep watch.

At that moment, the cult statue of Spes spoke. In a little girl's voice she dramatically proclaimed: 'Hope will blossom when Ostia picks the crocus.'

Lupus stared at the statue open-mouthed. Some people gasped and others began to praise the gods.

Three places in front of him the matron fainted. The aedile leapt to his feet and the bored guard fell to the ground in worship.

'Silence!' cried the aedile. 'Silence! Let the statue speak.'

A hush fell over the dozen or so people in the cella and they all looked expectantly at Spes.

'Hope will blossom,' repeated the statue, 'when Ostia picks the crocus.'

Lupus found his friends standing in the long queue of people lining the Decumanus Maximus. It was an hour before noon and it was hot.

'Lupus!' cried Flavia. 'Everybody is saying the statue spoke again. Is it true?'

He nodded and took out his wax tablet. However, before he could begin to write, they all heard Praeco the town crier: 'THE STATUE OF SPES HAS SPOKEN AGAIN: "HOPE WILL BLOSSOM WHEN OSTIA PICKS THE CROCUS".'

Lupus nodded and pointed at Praeco, who was walking down the street blaring out his news.

'She said that?' breathed Flavia. Lupus nodded again.

'IF ANYONE HAS AN INTERPRETATION,' cried Praeco, 'THEY SHOULD INFORM THE AEDILE, MARCUS SAFRONIUS RUFUS.'

'Did statue really speak?' asked Nubia.

Lupus nodded, then shook his head, then

shrugged and turned his palms to the sky as if to say: I don't know.

'HOPE WILL BLOSSOM WHEN OSTIA PICKS THE CROCUS!' blasted Praeco, and the four friends put their fingers in their ears as he came abreast of them. When he had passed beyond them, Flavia unplugged her ears in time to hear '. . . SAFRONIUS RUFUS.'

'Safronius must be the name of the magistrate we saw this morning,' she murmured.

Lupus nodded and wrote: HE AND HIS SCRIBE WERE THERE WHEN THE STATUE SPOKE.

Nubia tapped Flavia's shoulder. 'He has same name as that man.' She pointed to some graffiti on a pilaster between two shops.

Flavia read the graffiti: 'The muleteers urge the election of M. Artorius Bato as Pontifex Volcani.'

'No,' said Nubia. 'Below that one.'

'Oh,' said Flavia, and read the graffito below it: 'The bakers ask you to elect the aedile Marcus Safronius Rufus as Pontifex Volcani. Yes, that's the same person. He is an aedile.'

Lupus guffawed and pointed at the lowest slogan on the wall: 'The petty thieves of Ostia support Gamala.'

'I think that last one is a fake,' said Jonathan with a chuckle. 'The handwriting is the same as the one above it.'

Flavia looked at them: 'Aristo mentioned there

were some elections coming up. The first ones in nearly ten years.'

'Safronius is strange name,' said Nubia. 'I am never hearing it before.'

'It means "saffron", I think,' said Flavia. 'People with that name probably had ancestors who grew saffron and – great Juno's peacock! I've just figured out the statue's cryptic message!'

'What?' they all cried.

Flavia pointed to the graffiti. 'Right there,' she said. 'The answer is right there on the wall in front of us!'

'Aristo!' cried Flavia, running into the atrium. 'Are some elections about to be held here in Ostia?'

'That's right,' said Aristo, looking up from reading a scroll. 'The Pontifex Volcani died last week and they need to elect a new one. It's a lifetime position,' he added, 'the most honorable an Ostian can receive.'

'What is Pontifex Volcani,' asked Nubia.

'He's the chief priest of the cult of Vulcan,' said Flavia.

'Vulcan is the god of arms and armour, fish and fire,' added Jonathan. 'Remember how we celebrated the Vulcanalia last summer, right before Vesuvius erupted?'

Nubia nodded.

'Vulcan is Ostia's most important deity, of course,'

said Aristo, 'because he guards the granaries from fire. His chief priest – the Pontifex – oversees all the temples here in Ostia. The old Pontifex Volcani was very well respected. And extremely rich.'

Jonathan scratched his curly dark hair. 'I can't remember there being any elections before in Ostia,' he frowned. 'When we lived in Rome there were, but not here.'

'That's because these days the magistrates are elected by the town council,' said Aristo, 'the one hundred decuriones. But the Pontifex Volcani is still chosen by public vote.'

'Does that mean anybody can vote for Pontifex Volcani?' asked Flavia.

'Well, you and Nubia can't, because you're girls. Jonathan and Lupus can't, because they haven't come of age. Nor can I, being Greek. But any adult male Ostian who is a Roman citizen can vote.'

'When are the elections?' asked Jonathan.

'Day after tomorrow,' said Aristo. 'Six days before the Nones.'

'And who are the candidates?' asked Flavia.

Aristo grinned. 'Don't you read graffiti on the walls?' he asked.

'Pater always tells me not to,' she said primly. 'Some of it is rude.'

'Since when do you obey your father?' Aristo winked at Flavia.

'Is Lucilius Gamala one of the candidates?' asked Jonathan.

'That's right,' said Aristo. 'He's the favourite. His great grandfather was also Pontifex Volcani in the time of Augustus.'

Lupus held up his wax tablet. On it he had written: M. ARTORIUS BATO?

'Correct,' said Aristo with an approving nod. 'Our friend Bato is also a candidate.'

Nubia shyly raised her hand. 'Also Marcus Safronius Rufus,' she said. 'The aedile.'

'Nubia was the one who first spotted that graffito,' said Flavia loyally.

'And those are your three candidates,' said Aristo. 'Gamala, the favourite; Bato the possible runner-up, and Safronius, who is very young and doesn't really have much of a chance. He hasn't even finished serving out his year as aedile.'

'Then I think I know what the statue's message means,' said Flavia.

'You do?' Aristo raised an eyebrow.

'*Hope will blossom when Ostia picks the crocus,*' quoted Flavia, and explained. 'The "crocus" is Safronius, because saffron comes from the crocus flower. And when Ostia picks him means when Ostia elects him.'

'By Hercules,' said Aristo. 'Of course! It's so obvious. Why didn't I think of that?'

'May we tell the aedile?' said Flavia. 'The town crier told people to inform him if they could interpret the message.'

'But Safronius *is* the aedile,' said Jonathan.

'I know!' She looked round at her friends with bright grey eyes. 'When he hears this, maybe he'll give us a huge reward!'

Lupus tapped Flavia on the arm and held up his wax tablet.

WHAT IF IT IS A TRICK? he had written.

'He's right,' said Jonathan. 'You shouldn't just accept this, Flavia. Treat it like a crime. Do what you're always telling us to do. Find out who had the motive, means and method.'

'I have to agree with Jonathan,' said Aristo. 'That's not to say I don't believe a statue could talk, but we should rule out all other possible causes before we accept it.'

Flavia sighed and sat at the table. 'You're right,' she said. 'Let's treat this as a crime. If the statue *didn't* really speak, someone organized it to appear that way. Why?'

'Motive is obvious,' said Jonathan. 'Someone wants Safronius to be elected Pontifex Volcani. I'm betting Safronius himself.'

Aristo nodded. 'A position of honour and wealth, as I said. And if Flavia's interpretation of the oracle becomes known, then he will certainly win.'

'I admit that's a good motive,' said Flavia. 'But did Safronius have the means? And what was his method?'

'I'm not sure of the method,' said Jonathan slowly, 'or the means, but I think we should interview people who were in the temple when the statue spoke.'

Flavia nodded at him, then bellowed: 'ALMA!'

'Flavia Gemina!' cried Aristo. 'You know your father hates you bellowing like a fishwife.'

'Sorry!' said Flavia.

'Dear Juno!' cried Alma, running into the atrium with a wooden spoon in one hand. 'What's happened?'

'Nothing,' said Flavia sheepishly. 'We just wanted to interview you about this morning, when the statue spoke. Tell us who was there, what you saw, what you smelled, what you heard, anything that might help us . . .'

Alma sat down and put the spoon on the marble tabletop.

'Well, I heard that statue speak. I smelled the usual incense. As to what I saw . . . There were about ten or twelve other people there, mostly women. All women, now I think of it. I know most of them by sight. There was Claudia Hygia, and Scribonia Attica, and Sabina from the weavers' shop. That old fortune-teller from Ropemakers Street, oh, and the lady with the pet monkey who works in the fish-market.'

'Trimalchio the monkey!' cried Flavia. She laughed

and looked at Lupus. 'Remember we tried to give him to you as a present for your birthday last year?'

'But Trimalchio is running back home again,' said Nubia. 'With my scarab beetle having been eaten.'

'And after frightening away my talking bird,' said Jonathan.

Lupus grinned ruefully, and shrugged.

Suddenly, Flavia gasped. 'That's it!' she cried. 'I'll bet someone trained a parrot or mynah bird to utter the cryptic prophesy! They trained the bird to fly into the temple, perch on one of the ceiling beams and then utter the phrase upon a secret command.'

Flavia's friends nodded, but Aristo shook his head. 'Some birds can be trained to speak,' he said, 'but they're unreliable and don't always perform on command.'

'Besides,' said Alma, pushing back her chair and rising to her feet, 'that was no parrot. Don't you think I can tell the difference between a bird and a person?'

Flavia sighed. 'Fair enough,' she said. 'But how else could a statue speak?'

Suddenly Lupus sat bolt upright and looked round at them with bright green eyes.

'You think you know?' said Flavia.

A slow smile spread across Lupus's face and he nodded. Then he began to write on his wax tablet.

A few moments later, Nubia looked up. 'What is "ventriloquist"?' she asked.

'It's someone who speaks from the belly,' said Aristo, 'often without seeming to move their lips. The best ones can throw their voice across the room. Especially if the room is small and the acoustics are good.'

Flavia looked at Lupus. 'I think you've solved the mystery Lupus. And this is an excellent plan to prove it. The only problem is that our suspect knows who you are. I have a better idea.'

As the gongs clanged noon throughout the seaport of Ostia, a fair-haired girl walked down Ropemakers Street. A handsome young man preceded the girl, and a dark-skinned slave-girl followed humbly behind, holding a blue silk parasol to shade her mistress from the hot October sun. Presently the girl stopped at a shop with an Egyptian eye painted above the door and a crowd of feral cats on its threshold. The cats scattered as she rattled the bead curtain to get attention.

A moment later an old woman parted the beads and gazed out at them suspiciously.

'My name is Fulvia Pseudola,' said the girl imperiously. 'This is my pedagogue.' She waved dismissively at the young man. 'Are you Hariola the soothsayer?'

'I might be.' The old woman glared round at them with narrowed eyes.

'I would like,' said the girl, 'to contact the spirit of my older sister. She died last month.'

'Don't know if I can do that,' rasped the old woman. 'Not easy to get in touch with the departed.'

'If you help me speak to my older sister,' said the girl, 'I will give you this gold coin worth one hundred sesterces.'

The old woman's sour expression dissolved into a gap-toothed smile, and she pulled aside the bead curtain. 'Come in,' she said. 'Please, come in.'

Flavia looked round the soothsayer's booth. It was a tiny cube-shaped room at the front of an apartment block, hot and dim and barely large enough for the four of them. Sickly-sweet incense did not entirely mask the smell of blood and pigeon droppings.

A colourful cloth embroidered with hieroglyphs covered a round table. In one corner pigeons ruffled and cooed in a bamboo cage. In the corner opposite was a small stone altar, still messy with blood and feathers from an earlier sacrifice. Another corner was occupied by a small painted shrine, crowded with statuettes of the various gods and goddesses, and in the final corner glowered a large wooden statue of a dog-headed Egyptian god.

'It's good you're all here,' croaked Hariola. 'To contact a spirit of the dead we will need to make the mystic circle. Come, sit.'

In keeping with her disguise of a rich patrician girl, Flavia took the best seat and let Nubia and Aristo perch on stools. She hoped that by now the others would have taken up their positions outside in order to eavesdrop.

'Who is your patron god or goddess?' said Hariola.

'Diana,' said Flavia. 'Goddess of the hunt.'

'Good.' Hariola took a figurine of Diana and placed it at the centre of the table. Then the old woman shuffled over to the cage of pigeons. She took one out and murmured to it softly in a foreign tongue. Her murmuring became rhythmical and Flavia realized it was an incantation.

Next, Hariola laid the pigeon on the small stone altar, took up a bloody cleaver and chopped off its head.

A few moments later she returned to the table with a ceramic bowl of bright red blood. 'Spirits crave fresh blood', she explained. 'They lap at it like cats with a bowl of cream.' She placed the bowl carefully in the centre of the table, beside the statuette of Diana.

Hariola sat. 'What was your sister's name and how old was she when she died?'

'We called her Fulvia Prima and she was thirteen when she died,' said Flavia in her rich-girl's voice. 'I want to know where she hid my mirror.'

'Very well,' said Hariola. She dipped her

forefinger in the pigeon's blood and touched the foreheads of each of them. Flavia's shudder was not pretense.

'Now we must close our eyes and hold hands,' rasped Hariola, 'and I will try to make contact.' Flavia took Aristo's hand and felt Hariola's claw-like grip on her left. For a few moments the soothsayer uttered incantations and moaned softly. Flavia opened one eye a little to study her.

Flavia started as a girl's voice spoke behind Aristo.

'Fulvia,' said the girl's voice, 'this is your older sister speaking to you.'

Flavia gasped and Nubia uttered an involuntary cry.

'I am in the underworld,' said the girl's voice, 'but this wise woman called me back.'

Flavia opened both eyes to look at Hariola, whose own eyes were shut. How could she be making the girl's voice come from across the room? The old woman's mouth was closed, but Flavia thought she saw her neck twitching as the girl's voice continued: 'What do you want to know?'

'Um . . . I want to know,' said Flavia, 'where you hid the gilded mirror that Mater gave me. The one with Diana and her hounds etched on the back.'

'Look in my secret hiding place,' said the girl. 'You will find it there. And now: farewell.'

'Wait!' cried Flavia.

'The spirits do not linger long,' said Hariola in her

husky voice. 'But if you come back tomorrow I will summon your departed sister again.'

'You won't be here tomorrow!' cried a deep voice. The bead curtains rattled as a tall man stepped into the room. He had white hair and dark eyes, and his bearing was noble. Behind him stood two lictors, an official scribe, plus Jonathan and Lupus.

'Tomorrow,' he said, 'they will cut out your tongue for blasphemy and crucify you for deceiving the people.'

'Who are you?' cried Hariola. Her chair fell back as she leapt to her feet.

'My name is Publius Lucilius Gamala,' said the man, taking a step into the tiny room. 'I am a praetor of Ostia, and one of the candidates for the position of Pontifex Volcani.'

'I didn't blaspheme,' rasped Hariola, her face chalk white. 'I didn't do nothing!'

'Yes, you did!' said Flavia. 'You were at the Temple of Spes on both occasions when the statue spoke. And you've just proved you know the art of ventriloquism when you made a girl's voice seem to come from across the room.'

'That wasn't me!' cried Hariola. 'That was your dead sister.'

'I don't have a dead sister!' cried Flavia triumphantly. 'So admit it! Safronius paid you to make that statue speak, didn't he?'

'Curse you!' cried Hariola, shaking her bony fist at Flavia.

'In my capacity as praetor,' said Gamala, 'I hereby place you under arrest.' He nodded to the lictors, who stepped forward and seized Hariola by her bony arms.

'Curse you, too!' she screeched.

'If,' said Gamala, 'you confess the plot to my scribe, in the presence of these witnesses, then I will give you enough money for your passage back to Egypt. Agreed?'

Hariola stared down at the packed earth floor of her cubicle. Finally she lifted her wrinkled face and glared at them with her dark eyes. 'Agreed,' she said at last. 'I'm leaving this place and never coming back.'

'You've made a friend for life in Gamala,' said Aristo as they all walked back to Green Fountain Street. 'And he will be a most influential and valuable friend if he is elected Pontifex Volcani. With Safronius and his talking statue now discredited, I'm sure he will be chosen.'

'I wouldn't be too sure about that,' said Jonathan with a grin. 'He has some stiff competition.' Jonathan pointed at the white plaster wall of the fuller's shop they were passing.

In big, black charcoal letters, someone had boldly written:

I URGE YOU TO ELECT LUPUS
AS PONTIFEX VOLCANI!

—— AUTHOR'S NOTE ——

One night I was reading the Loeb edition of Martial's poems and I came across this one about a girl who is as beautiful as a statue, but who spoils the effect whenever she opens her mouth:

sed quotiens loqueris, carnem quoque, Lydia perdis
et sua plus nulli quam tibi lingua nocet.
audiat aedilis ne te videatque caveto:
portentum est, quotiens coepit imago loqui.

Here is my paraphrase:
Every time you speak, Lydia, you ruin your
    statuesque beauty
Your tongue does you more harm than anyone else's
    ever did.
Be careful the aedile doesn't hear that harsh voice while
    gazing on your beauty:
Because whenever a statue speaks, it's a portent!
Martial XI.102.5-8

It was the translator's footnote that caught my eye, and my interest:
'*It was the duty of the aedile to report all prodigies, such as a talking statue.*'

That's what gave me the idea for 'The Case of the Talking Statue'.

DEATH BY
VESPASIAN

This story takes place in February AD 81,
between book XIII, *The Slave-girl from Jerusalem*
and book XIV, *The Beggar of Volubilis*

(This is the rough draft of a letter written in February AD 81, in Ostia)

Marcus Artorius Bato, aedile of Ostia, to his excellency Titus Flavius Vespasianus, consul and first citizen of Rome: greetings!

I am writing in response to the letter you sent me last week, in which you asked me to report on the suitability of certain residents of this town to undertake a covert mission for you. You mentioned that although you had dealings with them last year you wanted to be brought up to date on their suitability for a mission to Asia or Africa. ~~I am honoured and humbled to be included in your plans O most excellent majesty. You are truly the prince of princes and worthy of the name Caesar.~~

As it happens, the four individuals under consideration have just helped me solve a rather gruesome crime here in Rome's great port. An account of the events will, I believe, convince you of their skill and ability to work as a team, if not of their willingness to travel halfway across our great Empire.

First, a brief summary of the four individuals in question.

Flavia Gemina. An eleven-year-old girl of the equestrian class. Her father is a sea captain, an unusual calling for a Roman of this class. Nevertheless, he is well-respected among the Ostian upper class, and among the plebs, too. Flavia is his only child, her mother having died in childbirth nine years ago. The father has never remarried. Flavia is extremely bright but also ~~irritatingly precocious~~ strong-willed, independent and passionate, with a ~~well-deserved~~ reputation for unorthodox behaviour. Despite this, she is also respected in the town, even popular. Last year she helped me restore nearly twenty kidnapped children to their parents, and Ostians of all classes are duly grateful to her for this. As her nomen suggests, she is a member of the Flavian clan, like yourself. ~~I believe this may help gain her loyalty to you personally~~. Physically she is unremarkable. She is rather tall for her age, with the typical Flavian colouring of light brown hair and grey eyes. She has good teeth and no outward blemishes. I can vouch for the fact that she has a strong constitution and is not susceptible to the illnesses that plague some travellers. Last year we travelled to Rhodes via Corinth and she was not ill once, except for some temporary seasickness during a bad storm, which affected us all.

Jonathan ben Mordecai. This twelve-year-old boy is more problematic. As you know, he is a Jew. There are rumours that he and his family also follow the teachings of a certain rabble-rouser named Chrestus, but this might be used to our advantage as Chrestus encouraged submission to authority. The problem with this boy is that he was implicated in last year's terrible fire in Rome. It is good that you are already aware of this fact. As you said in your letter, this may be used to secure his loyalty. If it were to become widely known that he was responsible for nearly 20,000 deaths . . . well, I shall draw a veil.

Physically he is also unremarkable. The usual Jewish features: olive skin, brown eyes, dark hair: curly in his case. And of course he is circumcised. This last detail could prove useful if you want him to infiltrate certain groups of people in North Africa or Asia Minor. ~~If you told me more about the mission you have in mind for these children, then I might be able to offer more specific advice.~~ Jonathan ben Mordecai is in good physical condition, apart from a tendency to suffer asthma attacks which can be quite severe. I witnessed one such attack on board ship, in which he almost died. However, his friends provided the proper remedy and he recovered. I might add that if you were ever to wish him to 'go to Hades', his asthma would make a good pretence for an early demise.

Nubia, freedwoman to Captain Geminus. I believe this girl was bought by Captain Geminus as a personal slave for his daughter in the summer of your accession to the throne. The African girl is an extremely attractive specimen, with dark skin, golden-brown eyes and even white teeth. She is of good constitution and – like the others – survived last year's fever. She is twelve years old and therefore of marriageable age. However, judging from her appearance, she has not yet reached physical maturity. She is a skilled musician and also gifted with animals. During the Saturnalia last year she subdued a ravening lion single-handed, using no other weapons than a cloak and her bravery.

Lupus. This boy is nine or perhaps ten years old. He is well-known to residents of Ostia because for several years he was one of its denizens, living wild among the tombs and begging in the forum. Recently, however, Fortuna has smiled on him. Last year he was left a sizeable inheritance and he is now a wealthy ship-owner. His guardian is the Jew Mordecai ben Ezra, Jonathan's father. The fact that Lupus owns a ship could work in your favour if you require the four children to undertake a sea voyage. Lupus has expressed a desire to become a merchant and sometimes employs Captain Geminus to pilot his ship and manage his business affairs. Physically the boy is in good shape, apart from one extraordinary defect. He has no tongue. This, however, has proved of remarkably little hindrance to him, as he has recently acquired the skill of being able to read and write both Latin and Greek. In fact, his inability to speak could even prove to be an asset. Dumb people are often considered deaf. Lupus could use this to his advantage, pretending to be deaf as well as dumb and perhaps overhearing vital clues.

It should be mentioned that these four children are fiercely devoted to one another, a strong argument in their favour. If you could command similar devotion from them, you would have won four very useful allies. As you yourself have pointed out, the very fact that they are children also makes them excellent candidates for spies. After all, who would suspect mere children to be your agents? ~~I suppose this is why you have them in mind for the mission, rather than a much more experienced person, like myself.~~

An example of their resourcefulness can be illustrated by the intriguing case ~~they~~ we solved last week. As promised, I will give a short account.

A few days ago I was receiving my clients as usual in the atrium of my new house on Green Fountain Street. (I was recently paid a very respectable amount of money for services provided in a court-case.) My new townhouse is only three down from the house of Jonathan and his family, which is in turn next door to that of Marcus Flavius Geminus and his daughter.

As you may or may not know, Ostia's southern town wall is currently being converted into an extension of the aqueduct. On this particular morning, workmen were banging and shouting, as workmen do. The noise became quite unbearable at one point, and so I took my last client of the day out onto the front porch. I was just bidding him farewell when the girl Flavia Gemina ran past in a most undignified manner, her hair flying and her palla flapping. She began banging the door knocker of the Jew's house. Her two dogs came hot on her heels, and the young freedwoman Nubia took up the rear.

Neither my client nor I intended to eavesdrop, but Flavia's voice was so loud that, as the door opened, we clearly heard her utter a most remarkable statement: 'Drowned in urine, Jonathan!' she cried. 'A man's been drowned in urine!'

Naturally I was intrigued by this utterance and asked my client, Aulus, to find out what she meant. Aulus walked casually along the pavement towards them, and as he drew near the open doorway, he knelt and pretended to tie a loose sandal strap. Just before the door slammed shut, Aulus heard Flavia say, 'At the Fullonica of Fabius near Pistor's bakery. They found him with his head in a vespasian!'

At this point, Excellency, I must ask you to forgive my use of such a crude term. I mean no disrespect to you or your esteemed brother or your deified father. Just because your father – may Jupiter bless his memory – set a tax on urine does not justify the mob's cruel use of his name as their pet term for the pot that men pee into. However, the use of the word 'vespasian' rather than 'pisspot' is crucial to this particular case and will become apparent as I unroll the mystery.

Aulus hurried back and told me what Flavia had said. Without wasting a moment, the two of us hurried to the Fullonica of Fabius. There we found a crowd of people gathered in front of the fuller's shop. Aulus is a big man so I let him lead the way through the crowd.

You know, of course, that most fullers leave pots outside for men to urinate into, and you know that the fullers then use this liquid as bleach for fabric. Well, on the pavement outside this fuller's was one such "vespasian". A big man wearing a patrician's tunic seemed to be kneeling in front of it. But as Aulus and I came closer we recoiled. The man's head was immersed in the jug and the foul yellow liquid had overflowed to make a putrid puddle around its base.

'Who is he?' cried one woman.

'Don't know,' replied a man. 'Never seen him before in my life.'

'How did this happen?' cried M. Fabius Nitidus, the owner of the establishment. He was wringing his hands and gazing down at the body. 'Oh, why did this happen to me?' Two thin boys with yellow-stained legs – probably his slaves – stood beside him. Further back was a woman with a hedgehog skin in her hand; I presume she had been brushing the togas and pallas which hung outside the shop. Another slave stood in the open doorway. He was coated with a dusting of pale grey fuller's earth and resembled a walking statue. All four of them looked at their master and shook their heads.

Fabius looked up. 'Did you two see anything?'

Following his gaze, I saw two more youths looking down from the roof. From the strong smell of sulphur I deduced they were smoking the cloth, and indeed, I could see the very tops of the tortoise-shaped frames over which they had stretched the togas.

'No, master,' one of them called down. 'We only just heard the commotion.'

'Hey!' cried the other one, pointing. 'That man down there has his head in a vespasian.'

At this point the Jew arrived – that is, Jonathan's father. He rushed forward, crying out: 'Stand back, I'm a doctor.' The four children were close behind him, with their pack of dogs.

'Master of the Universe!' The Jew pulled the man's head out of the pot and glared round at them. 'Why didn't any of you help him?'

(I must comment at this point that I was shocked by the Jew's appearance. I had seen him at a court case a few months earlier and he had looked quite respectable, almost Roman, in fact. Since then some calamity must have come upon him. He was thin as a spear, with a scraggly beard, unkempt hair and red-rimmed eyes.)

'I think he's been dead for a while, Father,' Jonathan said. 'He's frozen in that position.'

And indeed, the boy was right. Mordecai had eased the corpse gently down onto the pavement. It lay there on its side, frozen in a grotesque act of kneeling. Now we could all see the dead man's face; his eyes bulged and his tongue protruded in a most unpleasant way.

Flavia and ~~her slave girl~~ the freedwoman Nubia screamed and averted their eyes along with many others in the crowd. But the mute boy – Lupus – moved forward and actually brought his face closer to the dead man's. Suddenly he grunted and stood up again, and took out the wax tablet he always carries with him – it is his main method of communication – and scribbled something upon it.

I took charge at once. As you may know, I was aedile last year and hope to achieve the rank of praetor in the near future. 'What's going on here?' I said, and stepped forward. This allowed me to catch a glimpse of what the mute boy had written on his tablet: I KNOW HIM

'Greetings, Marcus Artorius Bato,' Jonathan

said respectfully. 'It seems this man drowned in a vespasian.'

(At this point I must add that Jonathan has changed, too, but for the better, not the worse. ~~His eyes had lost their hunted look and he seemed to possess a certain sense of calm authority~~.)

'Do you know this man?' I asked.

Lupus nodded and wrote on his tablet: I'VE SEEN HIM IN ROME

'Where in Rome? Who is he?'

Lupus frowned and chewed his lower lip, then shook his head. CAN'T REMEMBER he wrote, then pointed to the words above: I'VE SEEN HIM IN ROME

'He didn't drown,' an accented voice said.

The children and I turned to look at Mordecai. He was swaying very gently.

'What do you mean?' I asked him.

'His eyes are bulging and his tongue protruding,' the Jew said. 'He was strangled. But someone wanted to make it look as if he had drowned.'

I noticed Moredecai was slurring his words. Studying his face more carefully, I observed that his pupils were dilated. If I did not know better, I would say he had been indulging in some opiate.

'Do you have any idea when he died? Or where he was killed?' I asked him.

'At least eight hours ago. It takes that long for rigor mortis to set in. Also, his body is stone cold.'

'And yet,' Flavia said, 'the murderer can only have put his body here in the last hour or so.

'How do you come to that conclusion?' I said.

Without looking at me, she gestured to the bakery across the intersection, now closed for the day. 'Pistor shuts up shop about an hour before noon,' she said, 'and it's almost noon now. If the body had been put here when the shop was open, then somebody would have seen it. But nobody did. Therefore the body must have been put here in the last hour.'

'Brilliant!' I said and smiled approvingly at her. I had come to the same conclusion but wanted to hear her reasoning.

~~She ignored me. Perhaps she is still angry that I gave a very honest appraisal of her character in a court case last December.~~ 'That means Doctor Mordecai is right,' Flavia said. 'That poor man was murdered somewhere else and much earlier. If he had been drowned within the last hour his body would still be floppy. Also, the overflow of urine is still wet. It hasn't had time to dry. I would say the body was only put here within the last third of an hour.'

'Excellent deduction,' I said to her.

'Doctor Mordecai,' Nubia said. 'What is wrong?'

I turned to the Jew and saw that he was weeping. Silent tears were pouring down his face and running into his beard.

Jonathan took his father's arm. 'Come, Father,' he

said. 'Let's go home. There's nothing you can do for him now.'

'We'll see you back at your house,' Flavia said to Jonathan, 'I just want to find out more about this crime.'

As Jonathan began to lead his father home, other people started to go, too.

~~Flavia glared at me and said. 'Why don't you find out if the person who discovered the body is still here?'~~

I had to act fast. 'Who was the first to find him?' I asked in my most authoritative voice.

~~There was no reply.~~

~~'Offer a reward,' Flavia said under her breath.~~

~~'Ten sesterces to the person who first found the body!'~~

'Me!' three voices said, and three hands shot up.

Two vigiles stepped forward. I know most of the vigiles in Ostia but a new contingent had just come down from Rome and I didn't know these two. The third person with his hand up was Cletus the town idiot.

I ignored the idiot and turned to the vigiles. 'Identify yourselves!'

'I'm Betilienus Antiochus,' said a short man with the hair burned off half his head, 'but everyone calls me Fax on account of I accidentally set fire to myself one time.'

'More than once,' grinned the other one, a big muscular man who might have been handsome but for his missing nose. 'I'm Scribonius Atticus,' he added. 'My nickname is Fungus.'

'Tell me what you saw,' I demanded.

'We found him about a quarter of an hour ago,' Fungus said in the distinctive nasal voice that noseless men often have. 'Found him just like he was when you got here.'

'Looked like he was doing homage to the vespasian,' Fax said. 'We thought he was playing a prank at first, having a laugh.'

Fungus elbowed Fax. 'Remember I said how maybe he was bleaching his teeth?' Both men laughed, as did some others in the crowd.

'So then I tapped him on the shoulder,' Fax said, 'but I got no reply.'

The crowd laughed again and I saw Lupus – the mute boy – laughing with them. However, Flavia and her slave-girl were not laughing. They were staring in horror at Fungus. Perhaps they'd never seen a man with no nose before, particularly such a fresh example as this. I felt it my duty to enlighten them.

'When an adulterer is apprehended in flagrante delicto,' I explained, 'the outraged spouse is within his rights to demand amputation of the offender's nose.'

Nubia looked at Flavia. 'What?'

'Fungus was caught with someone else's wife,'

Flavia whispered, 'and the husband cut off his nose as punishment.'

'Correct,' I said, and turned back to the vigiles. 'Did you see anybody else lurking about?'

'Just him,' Fungus said, and pointed at Cletus. 'I'll bet he did it. Probably killed the man and then robbed him.'

'No!' Cletus was trembling uncontrollably, as he always does, and a dribble of saliva ran down his chin. 'They were here first! Not me. I saw them bending over him.'

'We was tapping him on the shoulder,' Fax said. 'I told you we was trying to see if he was dead or alive. That's all we was doing.'

Suddenly Lupus grunted and pointed at the corpse. Then he wrote on his wax tablet.

I SAW HIM LAST YEAR IN THE IMPERIAL PALACE. WAITING WITH OTHER CLIENTS OF THE EMPEROR. I THINK HE IS A SENATOR.

I felt someone tugging my toga and looked down to see Flavia Gemina ~~glaring~~ smiling at me.

'Arrest them,' she said firmly. 'They did it.'

'Arrest whom?'

'Fungus and Fax, of course! It's obvious they committed the crime.'

I decided to let her explain her reasoning and said nothing.

'Look at their feet,' Flavia said.

'They're barefoot,' I replied. 'What of it?'

'The vigiles always march from Rome to Ostia barefoot, ever since the edict. Remember how during the reign of Claudius the marines demanded new boots and he decreed they march barefoot? Everybody knows that the vigiles only get issued with boots once they arrive here in Ostia.'

'Yes. Everybody knows that. So?'

'That means they just arrived from Rome within the last few hours. They didn't even have time to pick up their new boots.'

'And?'

She pointed at the corpse. 'He's from Rome, too. Fungus and Fax probably sent him an anonymous message asking him to come to a certain location here in Ostia, where nobody knows him. Maybe they said his wife would be here, meeting her lover. He took the bait and when he arrived they strangled him. But they wanted to humiliate him so they waited and then forced his head in a vessel named after his patron. Titus is called Vespasian, too, you know.'

'But what motive would they have to kill him in such a humiliating way?' I persisted.

Flavia put her hands on her hips and shook her head. 'It's as plain as the nose on your face,' she said. 'Fungus was obviously sleeping with the senator's wife.' She glared up at me. 'If someone cut off *your* nose wouldn't you want revenge?'

I nodded.

'But Fungus needed his friend Fax to help him,' Flavia continued. 'That senator is a big man. It would take two strong men to carry his body. Here in Ostia, nobody would look twice at two vigiles carrying the slumped body of a man. They're always arresting drunks and vagrants. Whereas poor Cletus couldn't drag that body two feet. Therefore,' she concluded. 'Cletus is telling the truth and those two are lying.'

Of course, I had come to the same conclusion. I merely wanted to hear her reasoning.

'Arrest them!' Flavia said.

Fungus and Fax looked at each other, then began to run down the street.

'Arrest those men!' I commanded.

But there were no other vigiles about.

'Scuto! Nipur! Seek the thieves!' cried Nubia.

Instantly the two dogs were off like arrows from a bow, streaking after the fleeing pair. The whole crowd ran after them. We pursued them down Baker's Street towards the Green Fountain where they suddenly veered right. As we rounded the corner in a mass, we saw Fungus and Fax lying on the ground. With a certain poetic justice, it seems they had tripped over a vespasian on the corner of Fuller's Street. They lay groaning among broken terracotta in a spreading puddle of urine. The two dogs stood over them, wagging their tails.

'Ten sesterces to any man who helps to hold them fast,' I cried.

Needless to say we apprehended the two culprits and they confessed soon after.

I hope my modest account of this incident has shown you how resourceful the four children are and how well they work together. I heartily recommend that you send them ~~far, far away~~ on the mission to Asia, Africa or beyond.

I remain, as ever, your loyal client, servant and subject.

Vale.

— AUTHOR'S NOTE —

I got the idea for this story after a fan emailed me to ask what a fuller's, or *fullonica*, was. I thought it would be interesting to have a crime set in a *fullonica* so that I could explain a little about the ancient Roman way of cleaning clothes while Flavia solves the mystery. I originally wanted to call this mini-mystery 'Death by Urine' but my editor, Jon, objected. So I've called it 'Death by Vespasian'. I also thought it would be fun to have a story told from the point of view of someone else, so that we see the children from another angle. Finally, I wanted to set up the next few books, in which the four friends will travel to North Africa and Asia Minor on a mission for the Emperor Titus.

I learned about the barefoot Ostian vigiles from Suetonius, about noseless adulterers from the poet Martial, and about fullers' shops from Pliny the Elder.

ARISTO'S SCROLL

aedile (eye-*deal*)
  is a type of junior magistrate or town official
amphitheatre (*am*-fee-theatre)
  an oval-shaped stadium for watching gladiator
  shows, beast fights and the execution of criminals
Asia
  means Asia Minor or modern Turkey
atrium (*eh*-tree-um)
  the reception room in larger Roman homes, often
  with skylight and pool
Augustus (awe-*guss*-tuss)
  Julius Caesar's adopted nephew and first emperor
  of Rome, died in AD 14
barbiton (*bar*-bi-ton)
  a kind of Greek bass lyre, but there is no evidence
  for a 'Syrian barbiton'
cavea (ka-*vey*-uh) the shell-shaped seating area of a
  Greek or Roman theatre
Corinth (*kor*-inth)
  one of the most important cities in the Roman
  province of Greece, notorious for its lax morals
  and beautiful priestesses of Aphrodite

decurion (day-*kyoor*-ee-on)

   Ostia's city council was composed of 100 men called decurions; they had to be freeborn, rich and over 25 years of age

Domitian (duh-*mish*-un)

   son of Vespasian and younger brother to the Emperor Titus

duovir (doo-*oh*-veer)

   one of the two most important magistrates in Ostia, he served for a year and could preside as the chairman at trials

euge! (*oh*-gay)

   Latin exclamation: 'hurray!'

eureka! (you-*reek*-uh)

   Greek exclamation: 'I've got it!'

fax (facks)

   is Latin for 'torch'

Flavia (*flay*-vee-a)

   a name, meaning 'fair-haired'; Flavius is the masculine form of this name

forum (*for*-um)

   ancient marketplace and civic centre in Roman towns

fullonica or fuller's shop

   is the place where fabric was cleaned and bleached

fungus

   is Latin for 'mushroom' or the melty bit of wax on the tip of a wick

gladiator
was a man trained to fight other men in the arena, sometimes to the death

greaves (greevz)
metal shin-guards; the Thracian and hoplomachus wore tall ones, the murmillo wore a single short one on his left leg

Hercules (*her*-kyoo-leez)
very popular Roman demi-god, the equivalent of Greek Herakles

hoplomachus (hop-lo-mack-uss)
type of gladiator armed like a Thracian with metal greaves over quilted leg-guards and a brimmed helmet, but fought with a round shield and short, straight sword

impluvium (im-ploo-vee-um)
a rainwater pool under a skylight in the atrium

Italia (it-*al*-ya)
the Latin word for Italy

Jerusalem (j'-*roo*-sah-lem)
capital of the Roman province of Judaea, it was destroyed in AD 70

Juno (*joo*-no)
queen of the Roman gods and wife of the god Jupiter

Jupiter (*joo*-pit-er)
king of the Roman gods, husband of Juno and brother of Pluto and Neptune

Kalends (*kal*-ends)

the Kalends mark the first day of the month in the Roman calendar

Medusa (m'-*dyoo*-suh)

mythical female monster with a face so ugly she turned people to stone

murmillo (mur-mill-oh)

type of gladiator who usually fought hoplomachus or Thracian; he had a protected right arm and left leg, a big, rectangular shield, brimmed helmet and short sword

Nero (*near*-oh)

Emperor who ruled Rome from AD 54-69

nomen (no-men)

is the part of a citizen's name that tells what clan they are from; in men it is the middle name, in women the first of their two names

Nones (nonz)

7th day of March, May, July, October; 5th day of the others, including December

nymphaeum (nim-*fay*-um)

originally the term for a shrine to water nymphs, by the first century AD this word had come to mean any large, decorated fountain

Ostia (*oss*-tee-uh)

port about sixteen miles southwest of Rome; Ostia is Flavia's home town

palla (*pal*-uh)
   woman's cloak, could also be wrapped round the waist or pulled over the head
Palladium (pa-*lay*-dee-um)
   Trojan statue of Pallas Athena mentioned in Homer's *Iliad* and Virgil's *Aeneid*
papyrus (puh-*pie*-russ)
   papery material made of pounded Egyptian reeds, used as writing paper and also for parasols and fans
peristyle (*perry*-style)
   a columned walkway around an inner garden or courtyard
Pliny (*plin*-ee)
   (the Elder) famous polymath and author who died in eruption of Vesuvius; his only surviving work is a Natural History in 37 chapters or scrolls
Pollux (*pol*-luks)
   one of the famous twins of Greek mythology (Castor being the other)
Pontifex volcani or 'Priest of Vulcan'
   was an important elected post in Ostia
posca (*poss*-kuh)
   well-watered vinegar; a non-alcoholic drink favoured by soldiers on duty
praeco (*pry*-ko)
   herald, town crier or auctioneer

praetor (*pry*-tore)
   imperial administrator who often acted as chairman in the law-courts
retiarius (ret-ee-*are*-ee-uss)
   type of gladiator who usually fought secutor; he wore manica and galerus on his left arm and fought with net, trident and dagger; his name means 'net-man'
rigor mortis
   is Latin for 'the stiffness of death'
scroll (skrole)
   papyrus or parchment 'book', unrolled from side to side as it was read
secutor (seck-you-tor)
   type of gladiator who usually fought retiarius; armed like a murmillo but his smooth tight helmet enclosed the head completely, apart from small eyeholes
sesterces (sess-*tur*-seez)
   are bronze coins worth about £1 in today's money
stola (*stole*-uh)
   a long tunic worn by Roman matrons and respectable women
stylus (*stile*-us)
   metal, wood or ivory tool for writing on wax tablets
tablinum (ta-*blee*-num)
   room in a Roman house where the head of the family usually receives friends and clients

Thracian (*thrace*-shun)

gladiator armed like a hoplomachus with metal greaves over quilted leg-guards and a brimmed helmet, but fought with a small, square shield and curved sword

Tiber (*tie*-burr)

the river that flows through Rome and enters the sea at Ostia

tiro (*teer*-oh)

novice or beginner

triclinium (trik-*lin*-ee-um)

ancient Roman dining room, usually with three couches to recline on

tunic (*tew*-nic)

piece of clothing like a big T-shirt; children often wore a long-sleeved one

Venus (*vee*-nuss)

Roman goddess of love, Aphrodite is her Greek equivalent

Vespasian (vess-*pay*-zhun)

AKA Titus Flavius Vespasianus, Roman Emperor who reigned between AD 69-AD 79; he was the father of Titus and Domitian

vespasian (pronounced as above)

slang term for 'piss-pot', so-called because the emperor Vespasian set a tax on urine

Vesuvius (vuh-*soo*-vee-yus)

famous volcano near Naples, which erupted on 24 August AD 79

vigiles (*vig*-il-laze)

were soldiers who patrolled Ostia and Rome for fire and crime

wax tablet

wax-coated rectangular piece of wood used for making notes

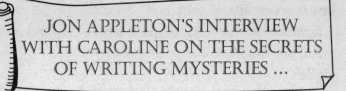

Jon: We know that your fascination with ancient Rome began when you were given The Last of the Wine *(by Mary Renault) and the* Iliad. *And we know that it was your sister who suggested you write a story for children set in ancient Rome. But where did the 'mystery' element come into play?*

Caroline: The mystery element came in because I used to love reading Carolyn Keene's *Nancy Drew* books. I think that was the first series that I really got hooked on as a child, and I must have read thirty of them. They're all pretty much the same, but I just loved being with Nancy and her friends solving mysteries, drinking cups of hot chocolate and things like that!

I think that the deeper, underlying motivation is that when you're an historian you're a bit of a detective yourself, because you're using the artefacts as clues, and you're using the written testimonies of the witnesses who lived two thousand years ago. You have to re-imagine the scene of the crime, as it were.

Jon: It seems lots of writers of historical fiction choose whodunnits and mysteries. What's the appeal of the combination of history and mystery?

Caroline: If books consist of plot, character and setting, then my main interest is in setting. I want to be transported to another world. I want to *be* there and smell it and taste it. *The Last of the Wine* took me back and made me smell and see and taste. One of the aspects of detective fiction is that it usually has a very strong sense of place and also of time. Whether you're Dashiell Hammett or Steven Saylor, you really have to depict the artefacts of that time because they're often important clues.

If the action story is the story of the hero who *fights* – the warrior – then the detective story is the story of the hero who *thinks*. Not everyone is a warrior, but we all think, and we all want to learn more about the world. I think that's the appeal of the detective story. Really, we're all just trying to figure out how to live in the world. In all of my books I consciously try to have a lesson for the characters.

Jon: So of your own books, do you prefer the ones that concentrate on the detection rather than the action?

Caroline: Actually, the ones I prefer are the romantic

ones: the hero who loves! Perhaps I'm a frustrated Mills and Boon writer. So my three favourites, are *The Pirates of Pompeii*, *The Twelve Tasks of Flavia Gemina* and *The Sirens of Surrentum*. They all have a mystery, but not that much action – the stories are about learning how to love. And in fact, even in the action books, what interests me most is what the characters learn at the end.

Jon: There's always lots going on in the Roman Mysteries. How do you develop them and how important is the mystery element?

Caroline: The mystery is only one of the ingredients, it doesn't take precedence. What I think about first is what I want the character to learn in the book and what their revelation will be near the end. So I decide what the character arc will be, and then what the setting is; the myth; the Roman topic that a Latin teacher could use (for example, love and marriage or slaves and freedmen); and the historical background (in one of my books I had Nero trying to kill his mother as the back story). Then I'll work out the mystery. The mystery is almost incidental, I'm afraid to say. Let's face it, there are really only two kinds of mysteries – The Whodunnit or Find the MacGuffin. (A 'MacGuffin' is Alfred Hitchcock's term for whatever the thing is in a story that people go after, like the Maltese Falcon or the Jewel of the Nile.)

Jon: Do you always know the villain's motivation and how they will be caught when you start a novel?

Caroline: I plan my books meticulously, building in all the plot beats that Hollywood script writers love. However, things can change. In the third book, I really intended for Felix to be behind it all the time but in the end I couldn't make him the baddie. Occasionally I'll be writing away happily and a door will open and a character I haven't planned will appear. Sisyphus, who's one of my favourite characters, was like that. I remember racing into the kitchen and saying to my husband, Richard, 'This character's just appeared who wasn't in my plot outline!' and then a few minutes later I ran back and said, 'He's taking over the investigation!'

In *The Beggar of Volubilis* I knew from the title that I had to have a beggar in it and for a long time I thought I knew who the beggar would be, but then I did a 'subtext' course on the internet, and now the beggar will be someone else. They talked about planting ulterior motives and surprises. For me, writing my fourteenth book, this was great because it just opened it up and I realised I had the power for a lot more reveals and surprises.

When it comes to writing and planning, you've got two things working at the same time – the right brain which is the creative brain and the left brain which is the logical side. I plan the book out with my left brain but I leave enough leeway for my creative subconscious to come up with alternate behaviour and characters. I think my right brain knows instinctively how some characters will behave, so I don't have to plot out character too much. Sisyphus came out in my subconscious but he's very real – in fact, characters are more real if they come that way than if you construct them like a formula.

Jon: *Detective stories always seem to be told in the first person (partly because you can't reveal too much about the mind of the criminal). But you seem to enjoy a bit more freedom in the mini-mysteries – is that true?*

Caroline: Yes. The beauty of a mini-mystery is that I can experiment with things that might not work in a fifty-thousand word book. 'Death by Vespasian' is written from the point of view of Marcus Artorius Bato, the junior magistrate of Ostia who is an ambivalent character, because we think he's on our side but he's actually corruptible. He sees the four detectives as annoying little pests – so that was great fun to write.

'Jonathan VS. Ira' is written in the first person, which I like doing, but the problem with it is you restrict yourself so much. The reader has to discover things exactly when your hero discovers them. The beauty of doing third person from four characters' point of view is that maybe Lupus can find out something and Flavia finds out something and *we* can put them together before the four detectives do.

Jon: For you as a reader and a writer, what are the ingredients of a good mystery story?

Caroline: Something that you can't put down, that keeps your interest all the way through. You want to see scenes played out rather than watch the black words on the page. When I lose interest in a book it's usually when it's not sensory enough – I'm just in the head not in the taste or the smell or the touch. In my own books, rather than fit in a whole block of description, I try to include one word in every phrase or every other phrase so the sights, smells and sounds are embedded in the story. I don't want readers to skip the descriptions. Also, I like it when you sense the writer isn't telling you everything and there's something more to learn. Audiences–readers –love the reveal, they *love* the surprise.

Jon: You've dedicated this book to Steven Saylor, who is best-known for his historical mysteries featuring Gordianus the Finder. We know you're a big fan of his work. Are there other mystery writers you'd recommend to anyone who enjoys the Roman Mysteries?

Caroline: Steven Saylor is absolutely brilliant. My mother, who has been a huge influence in my life, said she'd been enjoying his books, so I read them. It was after I'd written *The Thieves of Ostia*, so I was horrified to discover he has a little mute boy in one of his books. I met him last September and told him I hadn't stolen his idea when I created Lupus. I think he believed me. Steven really sets a sense of place and he brings in humour and surprise. I'd highly recommend him to readers, especially his collection of short stories called *The House of the Vestals*. (He's written a second collection called *A Gladiator Dies Only Once*). Also, I think that along with Arthur Conan Doyle, Agatha Christie is one of our greatest mystery writers. Many writers have stolen from her – and I have too, in *The Enemies of Jupiter*, for example, where it turns out the 'detective' did it. In another one of her mysteries there are twelve suspects and it turns out they *all* did it. Those are such a simple ideas, but they are *so* clever.

Jon: Do you have any tips or advice for fans wanting to create their own mini-mysteries?

Caroline: First of all, go on my website and look at my page of writing tips:
www.romanmysteries.com/characters/funsheet5.htm

I list seven plot beats which are very useful. Start with the criminal's motive and his modus operandi, and put in lots of good authentic Roman clues and make sure you've done your research. Don't e-mail me – do your research in the library or on the internet! The Cambridge Latin Course is one of my best sources of ideas and information. I've got ideas for a lot of my characters from that, because they use real people, like Sorex and Actius, the actors in *The Pirates of Pompeii*, whom we know about from graffiti of the times.

Jon: Can readers look forward to more mini-mysteries in the future?

Caroline: Absolutely! Although *Trimalchio's Feast* fills in most of the gaps in the series so far, I'm sure I'll have lots more fun new ideas.

CAROLINE'S TOP FIVE
BACKGROUND RESEARCH BOOKS

1. *Handbook to Life in Ancient Rome* by Adkins & Adkins
2. *As the Romans Did* by Jo-Ann Shelton
3. *Pliny the Elder's Natural History* by our dear friend Admiral Pliny
4. *Lives of the Caesars* by Suetonius (better known to us as Tranquillus!)
5. *Cambridge Latin Course* by Lots of Clever Boffins

(For more info on this course, which you might use in your Latin classes, go here:
http://www.cambridgescp.com

And you can see more of my favourite reference (and other!) books here:
http://www.romanmysteries.com/author/refbookshelf.htm

THE FIRST ROMAN MYSTERIES
QUIZ BOOK

With quizzes based on *The Thieves of Ostia*, *The Secrets of Vesuvius*, *The Pirates of Pompeii*, *The Assassins of Rome*, *The Dolphins of Laurentum* and *The Twelve Tasks of Flavia Gemina*, Roman clothes and fashion, music and musicians, glorious food, picture puzzles and illustrated Aristo's Scrolls, whether you are a devoted fan of the series or simply fascinated by what life was like in first-century Rome, this quiz book will test your knowledge.

THE SECOND ROMAN MYSTERIES
QUIZ BOOK

Based on *The Enemies of Jupiter*, *The Gladiators from Capua*, *The Colossus of Rhodes*, *The Fugitive from Corinth*, *The Sirens of Surrentum* and *The Charioteer of Delphi*.

To find out more about Caroline Lawrence and the Roman Mysteries visit
www.romanmysteries.com